WARNING!

If you are a parent or a teacher or even if you're just over eighteen, put this book down now! You won't like it. You won't understand it. You will be totally grossed out by it.

The book is full of time-traveling butts, time-traveling butt-fighters, mutant butts, robobutts, buttmobiles, butt-guns, cocobutt-trees, Great White Butts, giant brown blobs, and humongous arseteroids. And, as if all this wasn't bad enough, it's also full of truly disgusting creatures like stinkants, buttantulas, poopasaurs, tricera-butts, tyrannosore-arses, giant mutant zombie blowflies, and the extremely unpleasant Stink Kong.

If you are shocked, confused, frightened, or offended by any — or all — of these things (which, of course, you are because you are an adult), please put the book down immediately and go find something more suitable for a grown-up. Like a book on needlepoint, for instance. Or mortgage rates. Or why children insist on reading books about prehistoric buttosaurs despite the availability of much nicer, more meaningful, and significantly more profound books (like *The Day My Butt Went Psycho!* and *Zombie Butts from Uranus!*, for exampl

If, on the other hand, yo   self vaguely amused, slightly curious,   any — or all — of the things tha   ed about, then by all means   ok. . . . Just don't say that you

The Publishers

ALSO BY ANDY GRIFFITHS

JUST ANNOYING!

JUST JOKING!

JUST STUPID!

JUST WACKY!

JUST DISGUSTING!

JUST SHOCKING!

THE DAY MY BUTT WENT PSYCHO!

ZOMBIE BUTTS FROM URANUS!

BUTT WARS: THE FINAL CONFLICT

WHAT BUTTOSAUR IS THAT?

SCHOOLING AROUND #1: TREASURE FEVER!

SCHOOLING AROUND #2: PENCIL OF DOOM!

SCHOOLING AROUND #3: MASCOT MADNESS!

SCHOOLING AROUND #4: ROBOT RIOT!

Visit Andy's website: www.andygriffiths.com.au

BUTT WARS!

THE

FINAL CONFLICT

ANDY GRIFFITHS

Scholastic Inc.

New York   Toronto   London   Auckland
Sydney   Mexico City   New Delhi   Hong Kong

ISBN 978-0-439-74750-9

Copyright © 2005 by Backyard Stories Pty Ltd
All rights reserved. Published by Scholastic Inc.
SCHOLASTIC and associated logos are trademarks and/or registered trademarks of Scholastic Inc.,
557 Broadway, New York, NY 10012.

12 11 10 9 8 7 6 5 4 3   10 11 12 13 14 15/0
40

Printed in the U.S.A.
First Scholastic printing, December 2005

*Dedicated to everybody
who has — or has ever had — a butt.*

CONTENTS

Prologue

And enormous butts will conquer the world and complete and utter devarsetation will follow. Giant brown blobs will rain down upon the Earth for forty days and forty nights. An evil stench will cover the land. And butts will rule the world again as they did in their glorious prehistoric past.

from *The Book of Buttageddon,* Chapter 3006, Verse 258, the Sir Roger Francis Rectum edition.

CHAPTER ONE

Blob

Zack Freeman looked up and realized that he was about to be squashed by a giant brown blob.

Oh no! he thought. Not a giant brown . . .

But that was all he had time to think before the giant brown blob crashed down on top of him — and everybody else gathered at the Butt-fighting Academy.

Zack, his butt, his parents, Eleanor Sterne, Silas Sterne, the Kicker, the Smacker, and fifty of the best and brightest butt-fighting recruits in the world.

All squashed.

All buried.

All completely giant-brown-blobbified.

CHAPTER TWO

Blobbified

It was a sad end to what had been the proudest and happiest morning of Zack Freeman's life.

Not only had Zack just arrived back on Earth after saving the world from a zombie butt invasion and rescuing his parents from Uranus, but he had also graduated from Silas Sterne's Butt-fighting Academy. In one hand he proudly held his basic butt-fighter's certificate, and in the other a special medal of excellence for his work in the butt-fighting simulator.

Unfortunately, however, none of the challenges Zack had faced so far — either real or simulated — had prepared him for giant-brown-blobbification.

He was in way over his head.

And sinking fast.

He shut his eyes.

He pinched his nose.

He held his breath.

And then he did . . . well . . . *nothing*.

There was nothing he *could* do.

He could hardly move.

The blob was too thick. And too dark . . . or rather, too brown. Pitch-brown.

He didn't know which way was up.

He didn't know which way was down.

North or south.

East or west.

Zack's mind was racing.

He didn't want to die.

Not yet, anyway.

And especially not inside a giant brown blob.

What if the giant brown blob set hard and became a fossil?

And what if he became a fossil inside the giant brown blob?

And what if one day in the future they dug it up, cracked it open, and found him?

He didn't want his body to be put in a glass case and displayed in a museum for schoolchildren to laugh at. "Eeerggghhh, yuck!" they'd say. "Blob-boy! Look at the disgusting blob-boy!"

Then again, perhaps that was better than *not* being found and having to spend eternity trapped inside a giant brown blob. . . .

Zack shuddered at the thought. With a mighty effort he brought his mind back to the present. He had to stop worrying about what *might* happen in the future and start focusing on what was happening to him *right now*.

And fast.

Zack smiled ruefully as he realized he was still clutching his butt-fighter's certificate. He'd been so proud to receive it, but in this situation a butt-fighter's certificate wasn't even worth the paper it was printed on.

Or was it?

Paper.

The word triggered something inside him — but what? What use was paper?

Suddenly an image of his grandfather flashed into Zack's mind. Percy Freeman — one of the world's first butt-fighters: the Wiper. Armed with only a few rolls of toilet paper and an enormous load of courage, he had wiped some of the deadliest butts on the planet.

Paper.

Wiper.

Even as Zack's oxygen-starved brain was shutting down, the two words forged a fragile, but lifesaving, bond in his mind.

Zack knew what he had to do.

He brought the piece of paper up in front of his face.

And started wiping.

CHAPTER THREE

Wipe!

Zack wiped.
He wiped hard.
He wiped fast.

He wiped harder and faster than he'd ever wiped before.

He wiped out a clear space around his head, opened his mouth, and took a deep breath. Sure, it was bad air, but it was a lot better than *no* air.

Feeling stronger and more hopeful, Zack gripped the certificate with both hands and began the powerful scoop-wipe that he'd learned at the Academy. At the same time he began to kick his feet. It was hard work, but it allowed him to begin tunneling slowly through the blob.

He still didn't know where he was going, but at least he was going somewhere.

He'd been tunneling for only a few minutes when he felt a small soft shape moving in front of him.

Although he couldn't see anything in the pitch-brown, Zack could feel that the shape was in fact a small hand.

Zack recognized it immediately. He reached forward and pulled the hand — and its owner — into his tunnel.

"There you are!" said Zack to his butt. "I thought I'd lost you!"

"Zack?" it said in a small voice. "What happened? Where are we?"

"A giant brown blob fell out of the sky," said Zack. "That's what happened. And we're trapped inside it."

"It wasn't my fault!" said Zack's butt. "I didn't do it! I swear!"

"Calm down," said Zack. "I know you didn't."

"Are we going to die?" said his butt.

"Not if I can help it," said Zack.

"Great," said his butt. "So we ARE going to die!"

Zack was beginning to wish that he hadn't found his butt. He'd forgotten just how annoying it could be.

"I don't want to die!" screamed his butt. "I'm too young!"

"Then stop complaining and DO something!" said Zack, shaking his butt.

"What?" it said.

"That's exactly what I'm trying to figure out," said Zack. "We can keep wiping, but there's no way of telling where we're actually going. We could be going around and around inside this blob forever."

"Until we die, you mean," said his butt.

"That's enough!" said Zack. "You're not helping, you know!"

"Sorry," said his butt.

But deep down Zack wondered if his butt was right.

He'd wiped and wiped and wiped, and there was still no sign of a way out.

"Zack?" said his butt, in a brighter voice. "Remember when we got caught in the crapalanche?"

"Yes," said Zack.

"We thought we were going to die then, too, didn't we?" said his butt. "But we didn't."

"Actually, we *did*," said Zack gloomily. "We went over the Brown River sewagefall. We were crushed to death on the rocks, remember?"

"Oh yeah," said his butt. "That's right . . . but that wasn't *real* — it was in the butt-fighting simulator. And we only went over the falls because the Kicker accidentally set the difficulty level on the training program too high. And anyway, what about the brown hole? That *was* real and we got sucked into that and didn't die."

"I'm not sure about that," said Zack.

"Not sure about what?" said his butt. "Not sure that the brown hole was real?"

"No," said Zack, "I'm not sure that we survived. I think there's a strong possibility that we died and went to, well, you know . . . *and this is it*!"

"That's not funny, Zack," said his butt.

"I'm not trying to be funny," said Zack. "Even if we do get out, what would be the point? We'll probably just get squashed by another giant brown blob. I thought that after everything we've been through, and everything we've done, the Earth would finally be safe. I was wrong. I now see there's no end to it . . . and there never will be."

CHAPTER FOUR

Fight!

So that's it?" said Zack's butt. "You're giving up?"

"I'm not giving up," said Zack. "I'm just accepting reality."

"What about your parents?" said his butt. "And Eleanor, and Silas Sterne, and the Smacker, and the Kicker? You're just going to abandon them all?"

Zack shrugged. "I already saved them all," he said. "Twice! It's their turn to save me. If they're even still alive, that is."

"Zack," said his butt, "do you still have the medal and the certificate they gave you at your graduation?"

"Yes," Zack said.

"You don't deserve them," said his butt.

"What do you mean?" said Zack. "I *earned* them."

"You really believe that?" said his butt. "You know as well as I do that they only gave them to you because they felt sorry for you."

"Shut up," said Zack.

"It's true!" said his butt. "They all laugh at you behind your back. Face facts, Zack: You're a total loser. And you always have been. You can't even control me, your own butt, let alone save the world!"

"Do you want an atomic power punch?" said Zack. "Because you're heading the right way to get one."

"Oooh, don't scare me," said his butt.

Despite the pitch-brownness, Zack saw red. Things were bad enough without having to put up with being taunted by a butt. Especially his own. He was going to teach it some respect, even if it was the last thing he did — which, by the way things were looking, it probably would be. He drew back his fist and let fly.

WHAM!

"Didn't even hurt!" said his butt.

Zack atomic-power-punched it again — this time with both fists.

POW!

The force of the punch sent his butt deep into the brown murk of the blob.

"Call that a double-handed atomic power punch?" said his butt's muffled voice. "You should be ashamed of yourself. Didn't they teach you anything at the Butt-fighting Academy?"

Zack launched himself forward and went after his butt with a bloodcurdling yell. "This is all your fault!" he screamed.

Zack punched.

Zack smacked.

Zack kicked.

Zack pinched.

Zack punched and smacked and kicked and pinched his butt with all the atomic butt-punching butt-smacking butt-kicking butt-pinching force that he could muster.

With every blow they traveled farther and farther through the blob.

Zack was still punching and smacking and kicking and pinching a few minutes later when he and his butt broke through the thick, dried outer crust of the giant brown blob and rolled onto the ground.

CHAPTER FIVE

Dig!

Zack lay on the ground blinking against the brightness of the day. He was caked with brown-blob sludge. The stench was awful.

"Haven't you two got better things to do than fight at a time like this?" said a voice.

But before Zack could reply — or even stand up — he felt a cold blast of water hit his body. He rolled around on the ground, helpless against the force of the icy torrent.

Finally, just when Zack felt he couldn't possibly get any colder or wetter, the water stopped.

As he lay there shivering, he saw a pair of boots step in front of his face. They were covered in sludge from the blob.

"Well, don't just lie there!" said their owner. "Get up and give me a hand!"

"Eleanor?" said Zack, wiping water from his eyes.

"No, it's the Easter bunny!" said Eleanor. "Who do you think?"

"You're not going to hose me again, are you?" said Zack, getting to his knees.

"I will if you don't hurry up," said Eleanor, still pointing the emergency butt-fighting hose at him. "Come on! There are people dying in there!"

"But how did *you* get out?" said Zack.

"Anti-giant-brown-blob spray," said Eleanor, producing a small can from her butt-fighting utility belt. "I never leave home without it!"

"Nobody told *me* about that," said Zack.

"You didn't ask," said Eleanor.

"I didn't even *know* about giant brown blobs!" said Zack.

"Well, you do now," said Eleanor, waving her hose at the blob in front of them. "But what you probably *don't* know is that they set hard in less than an hour. We've got to get everybody out before it's too late!"

"He'll be no use," said Zack's butt, shivering. "He's hopeless."

Zack bent down, picked up his butt, and cradled it gently in his arms. "Shhhh," he said. "It's okay. I know you just said all those things to get me mad enough to punch our way out of the blob. But you can stop now. We're out!"

"I meant every word, you butt-fighting wannabe!" said his butt, still punchy from the beating.

"We haven't got time for this!" said Eleanor, thrusting a shovel into Zack's hand. "You can sort this out later.

Meanwhile, we have people to save! Including your mother and father!"

Zack stared at the shovel and felt sick. Compared to the blob, the shovel seemed no bigger than a teaspoon.

There was no point even starting.

But he couldn't just let his parents die!

Not when he was just getting to *really* know them. He'd always believed that they played in the wind section of a symphony orchestra that toured all over the world. He'd had no idea it was a cover for their real work as top secret butt-fighting agents. And he sure hadn't gone to all the trouble of traveling to Uranus and back to rescue them just to lose them to a stupid brown blob.

Zack attacked the blob with his shovel.

Eleanor blasted the blob with her hose.

But it was tough going.

After ten minutes Zack was exhausted. The blob seemed to be setting harder with every passing moment. He rested on his shovel, panting. The hole he'd made in the blob was pathetically small. "It's no use," he said.

"Keep digging!" said Eleanor. "We have to try!"

"It's impossible," said Zack.

"Give me one good reason *why*," said Eleanor.

"How about that one right behind you?" said Zack's butt.

Zack and Eleanor turned around slowly.

And gasped.

CHAPTER SIX

Surrounded!

There, towering over them, was the Great White Butt, the most evil and ruthless butt in the entire history of the world.

Zack felt his heart pounding.

There it stood. Two enormous white cheeks of pure menace — dedicated to nothing less than the down-fall of humanity — propped up by two skinny white legs.

"But that's impossible!" whispered Eleanor. "The Great White Butt was sucked into the brown hole!"

"So were we," said Zack. "But you know what? I don't think it *is* the Great White Butt."

"Of course it is," said Eleanor. "I'd know those cheeks anywhere."

"So would I," said Zack, "but those cheeks have no burn marks. No scars. No harpoon wounds."

"Um, Zack?" said Zack's butt.

"Not now," said Zack.

"Yes, *right now*!" said Zack's butt. "Look behind you."

Hardly daring to take their eyes off the Great White Butt, Zack and Eleanor nevertheless turned around slowly to see something that neither of them could believe.

Another Great White Butt!

"*Two* Great White Butts?" said Zack, looking from one to the other rapidly. "But I thought there was only *one*."

"Three to be precise," said Zack's butt, as a shadow passed over them. "Look to your right."

Zack and Eleanor, almost beyond shock now, looked to their right. There, sure enough, blocking out the sun, was a third Great White Butt.

Nobody said anything.

They didn't know what *to* say.

Zack's butt broke the silence. "Actually, better make that four altogether," it said. "Look to your left!"

Zack and Eleanor did not want to look to their left. But look to their left they did, to see a fourth Great White Butt approaching them.

The two butt-fighters now stood back to back and turned slowly as they watched Great White Butts advancing on them from all sides.

The ground was shaking.

Zack's butt leaped into his arms. It was shaking even harder than the ground.

"What do you think this means?" said Zack, trembling

in spite of the fact that he was a fully qualified butt-fighter with a special medal for excellence in simulated butt-fighting.

"Well," said Eleanor, "I'm just guessing, but I'd say it means we've got a butt-fight on our hands."

CHAPTER SEVEN

Butt-Fight

You've got to be joking, Eleanor!" said Zack, as the Great White Butts closed in on them. "We can't possibly fight *four* Great White Butts!"

"Well, what do you suggest we do?" said Eleanor. "The hokey pokey?"

"It worked on the zombie butts," said Zack.

Eleanor rolled her eyes and stepped forward. "Which one of you is the Great White Butt?" she shouted at the butts.

"Here!" boomed the Great White Butt directly in front of her. "I'm the Great White Butt."

"No, I'm greater than you," said the Great White Butt to her left.

"But I'm the greatest!" said the Great White Butt to her right.

"No, I'm greater than the greatest!" insisted the fourth.

Zack tried to block his nose. The gales of methane emitted as the four Great White Butts argued among themselves were almost worse than the stench of the giant brown blob.

"That's enough!" yelled Eleanor ferociously. "I'm not in the mood for this."

The four Great White Butts stopped their argument immediately. Even Zack felt scared. Eleanor was pretty frightening when she was angry. Even if you were a Great White Butt. Even if you were greater than the greatest of the Great White Butts.

"Listen to me," said Eleanor, turning slowly as she spoke in a low, murderous voice. "To tell you the truth, I don't care which of you is the Great White Butt. What I really want to know is, which one of you is responsible for *this*?"

Eleanor pointed at the giant brown blob.

The four Great White Butts were silent.

"Well?" said Eleanor, her eyes flashing.

"He did it!" said the Great White Butt in front of her, pointing to the one at her left.

"No, I never!" said the accused Great White Butt, turning a deep red and then pointing to the Great White Butt at her right. "It was him!"

"Liar!" said the Great White Butt at Eleanor's right, pointing at the Great White Butt behind her. "It was him!"

"No, it wasn't," said the Great White Butt behind her. "It was him!"

Eleanor looked at where it was pointing.

It was pointing at Zack's butt.

"How could *I* have done it?" said Zack's trembling butt. "Look at me! I'm tiny!"

"You are *now*," said the first Great White Butt. "Better out than in, I always say."

The Great White Butt burst out laughing at its little joke. The others joined in.

"Right," said Eleanor, not impressed. "That does it. Now you're all going to pay. Zack, you and your butt hit the deck. Now!"

Zack and his butt did as they were instructed.

Eleanor whipped out a Nail-rifle XR-5000 from her butt-fighter's belt, dropped to one knee, and spun in a fast circle, spraying the Great White Butts with a double-barreled burst of six-inch reinforced tungsten-tipped roofing nails.

"Ouch!" said the Great White Butt in front of her.

"Double-ouch!" said the Great White Butt at her left.

"Triple-ouch!" said the Great White Butt at her right.

"Ouch! Ouch! Ouch! Ouch!" said the Great White Butt at her rear.

"Don't you mean 'quadruple-ouch'?" said the first Great White Butt.

"I'll be the judge of what I'm feeling," said the rear butt, letting fly a giant brown blob at the butt in front.

Eleanor and Zack shielded their faces with their hands. SPLAT!

It was a direct hit, and pieces of fresh giant brown blob splattered everywhere.

The other Great White Butts laughed.

"Find that funny, do you?" said the freshly hit Great White Butt. "Well, laugh it up, funny-boys!" And so saying, it launched two giant brown blobs at the giggling butts.

Suddenly the air was alive with giant brown blobs flying in all directions as the four Great White Butts pounded each other in an earsplitting, nostril-burning free-for-all.

"Come on!" said Zack, putting down his butt and picking up his shovel.

"What are you doing, Zack?" said his butt.

"We've got to get the others out!" said Zack. "Before it's too late!"

"It already *is* too late," said Eleanor sadly. "The blob will have set hard by now."

"No!" said Zack. "My parents are in there!"

"I know, Zack," said Eleanor. "So is my father. But there's nothing we can do for them now. All we can do is save ourselves and keep fighting. It's what they would have wanted."

Zack looked at the blob. He looked at Eleanor. He knew she was right, but he still couldn't bring himself to leave.

Eleanor grabbed his arm. "Get a grip, Zack," she said, pulling him away.

CHAPTER EIGHT

Schlooomph!

Zack grabbed his butt and the three of them ran down the hill toward what remained of the Butt-fighting Academy.

Suddenly, all was quiet behind them.

"Uh-oh," said Zack, turning around. "I think they've noticed we're missing."

"How do you know?" said Eleanor.

Zack put out his hand and grabbed Eleanor, bringing her to a dead stop.

"Zack! What do you think you're . . . ?" she started, but then a giant brown blob smashed down right in front of her — right where she would have been if Zack hadn't stopped her.

"Thanks," said Eleanor.

"No problem," said Zack.

"Wrong!" said Zack's butt. "We've got plenty of problems. Look!"

The four Great White Butts had indeed stopped pounding each other and had turned their attention back to the butt-fighters. Four giant brown blobs were already flying through the air toward them.

SCHLOOOMPH!

A giant brown blob crashed down behind them.

SCHLOOOMPH!

A giant brown blob crashed down in front of them.

"Go left!" yelled Zack.

SCHLOOOMPH!

"Go right!" yelled Zack's butt.

SCHLOOMPH!

"Don't move!" said Eleanor.

They were surrounded. Again.

Zack, Eleanor, and Zack's butt huddled together.

Zack realized it would only be a matter of moments before they were buried beneath a fresh giant brown blob.

He sighed, closed his eyes, and blocked his nose.

CHAPTER NINE

Death Ray

They waited.
And waited.
And waited.
But the blob didn't come.

Zack peered out from underneath his fingers and looked back up the hill. He couldn't believe what he was seeing. "Hey!" he whispered to Eleanor and his butt. "Look!"

As the four Great White Butts prepared to launch a new round, another Great White Butt flew down out of the sky and landed behind them.

Only this one was even whiter than the others.

The four Great White Butts didn't appear to notice the new butt until it picked two of them up by the tops of their cheeks, swung them through the air, and smashed them together.

The butts fell limply to the ground.

"Wow!" said Zack's butt. "That's impressive!"

"Yeah," said Eleanor. "But why is it attacking its own kind?"

"Who cares?" said Zack's butt. "Let's run."

"Good idea," said Zack.

The butt-fighters seized their chance. They picked their way through the minefield of brown blobs and ran for the safety of the Butt-fighting Academy mess hall.

After dispatching the other two Great White Butts in a similar fashion, the whitest of the Great White Butts flew down toward the tiny butt-fighters and landed in front of them, blocking their way.

Eleanor drew her nail-rifle. "Eat six-inch reinforced tungsten-tipped roofing nails!" she yelled, firing off the few remaining rounds. But the nails had no effect. They simply made a metallic pinging sound as they bounced off the butt's shiny white hide.

The Great White Butt just stood there silently.

"I'm out of tricks," said Eleanor desperately. "What have you got, Zack?"

"This!" said Zack as he removed his medal and flung it, like a ninja star, at the Great White Butt's left cheek.

But the medal, like Eleanor's nails, bounced harm-lessly to the ground.

"That's it for me," said Zack. He turned to his butt. "You got anything?"

His butt emitted a short burst of gas.

"Pathetic," said Eleanor. "But thanks for trying."

Then the Great White Butt leaned down toward them.

"Nose-plugs on!" said Eleanor. "It's going to gas us!"

But instead of gassing them, the Great White Butt emitted a dazzling beam of bright white light.

"Aaagghh!" yelled Zack's butt. "I'm burning up!"

"Me too!" said Zack. "And I can't move!"

"Me neither!" said Eleanor, trying to cover her eyes with her jacket.

It was as if the light was sucking every bit of energy from their bodies.

So, thought Zack grimly, out of the frying pan and into the fire. They'd escaped from the horror of the brown blob — only to be cooked to a crisp by a Great White Butt's death ray.

Zack tried to shield his eyes from the glare, but as he brought his arm up to his face, he was amazed to see it become transparent and then disappear.

Zack looked down.

His whole body was disappearing.

Right in front of his eyes.

CHAPTER TEN

Ned

Everything went black.
But only for a moment.
Zack blinked.
And blinked.
And blinked again.

His eyes, still dazzled by the light, slowly adjusted to their new surroundings. Zack saw that he, his butt, and Eleanor were standing in exactly the same positions they were in when they'd been caught in the light.

The only difference was that they were now standing in the center of a glass cylinder in a room that was filled with computers, levers, pulleys, cogs, springs, dials, and wires. There was a bank of security camera–style screens on one wall transmitting grainy black-and-white images. Zack squinted, but was too far away to make out exactly what the images were.

"Teleportation complete," announced a soothing female voice.

Zack spun around to see who had spoken, but there was nobody there. The voice seemed to come from everywhere and nowhere at the same time.

"Teleported?" said Zack. "Are we *inside* the Great White Butt?"

"I guess so," said Eleanor, tapping the glass around them with a puzzled look on her face.

"Wow," said Zack. "I didn't know Great White Butts had control centers."

"There's a lot we don't know about Great White Butts," said Eleanor. "Including the fact that up to half an hour ago we thought there was only *one* of them. And that we thought we'd seen the last of it."

"I'm scared," said Zack's butt, hugging Zack's leg.

"Will you cut that out?!" said Zack.

"But I'm scared!" said Zack's butt.

"No need to be scared!" said a voice from behind them. "You're with friends now!"

Zack and Eleanor wheeled around.

A bearded man wearing a tattered butt-fighter's uniform and a big smile was standing in front of them.

CHAPTER ELEVEN

Robobutt

Ned?" said Zack. The last time Zack had seen Ned was when they were leaving his shack in the Great Windy Desert after he'd helped them to plug up a deadly buttcano. "Ned Smelly?"

"The very one!" said Ned, stepping forward to slide open the door of the glass tube and embrace his friends. Luckily the terrible body odor that had earned Ned his nickname was no longer evident. Well, at least it was no worse than any other retired butt-fighter's body odor. This was because Ned had given up his diet of needle-weeds and stinkants in favor of much less stinky anti-butt energy bars.

The three hugged.

"I came as soon as I could," said Ned.

"What are you talking about?" said Zack. "You've been swallowed by a Great White Butt! You have to go where *it* goes!"

Ned laughed. "Wrong," he said. "She goes where I tell her to go. Welcome to *Robobutt*!"

Zack looked at Eleanor.

Eleanor looked at Zack.

"Methane madness," they said in unison.

"No," said Ned. "Just a piece of inspired design and a lot of hard work. She's the ultimate butt-fighting machine. I built her out of the parts of crashed and abandoned butt-mobiles I found in the Great Windy Desert."

"Robobutt is a girl?" said Zack's butt. "Eerrgghh!"

"Yes, well . . ." said Ned. "It gets lonely out there in the desert. Introduce yourself, Robobutt."

"Hello. I am Robobutt," said the soothing female voice they had heard earlier. "Fully riveted reinforced steel cheeks. Turbo-assisted jet repulsion units. Nuclear wart-head equipped. Matter transport assisted entry and exit. Inside and outside voice options. Onboard tea- and coffee-making facilities. And I am self-wiping!"

"Well," said Ned, proudly. "What do you think?"

"Is this your idea of a joke?" said Eleanor.

"Joke?" said Ned, a little taken aback. "What do you mean?"

"Making us think that we were being burned up by a Great White Butt's death ray," said Eleanor. "That's what I mean."

"I'm sorry," said Ned. "But I couldn't think how else I could get you inside. Robobutt can broadcast her voice outside, but I hardly think you would have accepted an invitation to climb aboard. Please forgive me. And try to look on the bright side: You're now safe inside the ulti- mate butt-fighting machine. Not only can she travel across land, fly through the air, and swim through the sea, she can . . ."

"Ned," interrupted Eleanor. "I'm glad you're so happy with your new toy, but you're too late."

"What do you mean?" said Ned. "You're alive, aren't you?"

"Yes," said Eleanor. "But everybody else is dead. Half an hour ago a giant brown blob hit the open-air chapel. Everyone was squashed. Zack's parents. My father. The Kicker, the Smacker, and this year's entire intake of butt-fighting recruits."

"We're the only ones who got out alive," said Zack.

Ned shook his craggy, grizzled head that showed the scars and blast-marks of a lifetime of butt-fighting. "I'm afraid I have even worse news," he said softly.

"What could possibly be worse than that?" said Eleanor.

Ned didn't reply. He motioned them to follow him over to the bank of screens flickering on the far wall. "See for yourself," he said.

CHAPTER TWELVE

Buttageddon

Zack stood in front of the fifty-screen display and blinked. He'd never seen so many television screens at the same time. Or so much destruction.

One screen showed giant brown blobs pounding the pyramids of Egypt into rubble.

Another screen showed a gang of Great White Butts tearing the Eiffel Tower from the ground.

A third screen showed New York being swamped by giant waves of brown sludge.

It was hard for Zack to know which screen to look at.

It was even harder to make sense of the sheer scale of the unfolding disaster. All Zack knew was that it was impossible to look away.

"Zack?" said his butt. "I'm scared. Can you hold my hand?"

Zack took his butt's trembling hand in his as they watched the unfolding mayhem.

"This is for real?" said Zack.

"Yes," said Ned sadly. "Live via buttcam. Robobutt has access to satellites transmitting images from around the world twenty-four hours a day."

Zack clutched Eleanor's arm. He'd seen isolated towns ravaged by butt attacks before, but nothing on this scale. And he could tell, judging by the expression on Eleanor's face, that neither had she.

Buttquakes. Stink-tornadoes. Brown rain. Crapa-lanches. Vast armies of Great White Butts bent on giant-brown-blobbifying the entire world to buttblivion.

"Buttageddon," whispered Eleanor, as she stared open-mouthed at the nightmarish images on the screen.

CHAPTER THIRTEEN

Buttageddon?

Buttageddon?" said Zack.

"Buttageddon," said Ned, nodding solemnly.

"Oh no!" said Zack's butt. "Not Buttageddon!"

"Yes," said Eleanor. "Buttageddon."

CHAPTER FOURTEEN

Prophecy

Well, that's just great," said Zack. "Now that we've got that cleared up, would some-body mind telling me what Buttageddon actually is?"

"Affirmative," crackled Robobutt. "Buttageddon: The complete destruction of the world by butts. As prophe-sied in the ancient text *The Book of Buttageddon*, where it is written, 'And enormous butts will conquer the world and complete and utter devarsetation will follow. Giant brown blobs will rain down upon the Earth for forty days and forty nights. An evil stench will cover the land. And butts will rule the world again as they did in their glorious prehistoric past.'"

Zack gasped. "Did the ancient texts say anything about how to prevent it?" he said.

Ned shook his head sadly. "No," he said. "They just said it would happen."

"But how?" said Zack. "And why? Where did all these Great White Butts come from?"

"That I *do* know," said Ned. "One week ago I was in the Great Windy Desert hunting for stinkant juice. Robobutt uses it exclusively. It's the most powerful fuel source in the world. A single drop will take you around the world and back — but it's very hard to find. I'd been searching all day without much luck. I was about to head back when I felt a huge tug on the divining rod. It was stronger than anything I've ever felt before. Next thing I knew, the ground crumbled beneath me and I fell into what turned out to be an ancient stinkant nest. It was huge. I spent the better part of two weeks mapping it before I discovered a tunnel that led me to an enormous cave containing a vast reservoir of prehistoric stinkant juice. I filled my canisters and was about to leave when I noticed something written on the wall."

Ned paused here, apparently unnerved by the memory.

"What was written on the wall, Ned?" said Eleanor.

Ned pulled a crumpled notepad from his top pocket. "I wrote it down," he said. He flipped through the pages, took a deep breath, and began to read. " 'Warning! The Great White Butt is using the brown hole to send prehistoric Great White Butts forward through time. Stop him or the world is doomed.' "

Ned closed the pad and put it back into his pocket. "That's all it said. And underneath there were three skeletons, huddled together."

Eleanor looked skeptical. "Are you sure you weren't suffering methane madness down there?"

"It wasn't methane madness," said Ned. He reached into his pocket again and pulled out a bar of soap. "One of the skeletons was holding this."

Zack looked at the soap and gulped. *Imperial Leather* . . . his grandmother's favorite brand.

CHAPTER FIFTEEN

Soap

"Are you all right, Zack?" said Eleanor. "You've gone all white."

"That's my . . ." said Zack, finding it difficult to put what he was thinking into words. "That's my grandmother's soap. You know how fanatical she was about washing her hands."

Now it was Ned's turn to be confused. "Your *grandmother's* soap?" he said. "That's impossible, Zack. I carbon-dated that message. It was sixty-five million years old."

"Sixty-five million?" said Zack. "Are you sure?"

"Positive," said Ned. "I had Robobutt check the results."

"But that's crazy," said Zack. "How could my gran be writing sixty-five-million-year-old messages?"

"Beats me," said Ned, shrugging.

"Unless," said Eleanor thoughtfully. "Unless we

weren't the only ones who made it out the other end of the brown hole."

"You think Gran survived as well?" said Zack. "But we didn't see her on Uranus."

"Maybe she didn't go to Uranus," said Eleanor. "Maybe . . ."

"Hang on," said Ned, his mouth open in astonishment. "Are you saying that you got sucked into a brown hole and ended up on Uranus?"

"Yes," said Eleanor. "After the zombie butt invasion . . ."

"*Zombie butt invasion*?" said Ned, even more astonished than before.

Eleanor and Zack looked at each other.

"Ned," said Eleanor, "how long were you underground in that stinkant nest?"

"Hard to say," said Ned, frowning. "About two weeks, I think — I kind of lost track of time."

"Did you have any contact with the outside world while you were down there?" said Zack. "Radio? Buttcam?"

"Nothing," said Ned. "I was too far underground. What on earth happened?"

"It's a long story,"* said Zack, "but after the Great White Butt was blown out of the buttcano, he was flung through space and collided with Uranus. The collision created a huge explosion that caused a whole load of butts to turn into zombies, which then attacked Earth.

*For the full story see *Zombie Butts from Uranus!*, Andy Griffiths, Scholastic, New York, 2003.

We fought them off, but ended up chasing the Great White Butt back into outer space, where we were sucked into a brown hole, along with my gran — the Pincher — and two other butt-fighters, the Flicker and the Forker. We didn't know what had happened to them. Until now, that is."

"Let me get this straight," said Ned. "Are you saying that one of those skeletons might have been your gran?"

"It would certainly explain the soap," said Eleanor.

"And the message. The brown hole must have sucked her, the other butt-fighters, and the Great White Butt back to prehistoric times — when prehistoric buttosaurs ruled the Earth!"

"So you think the Great White Butt is using the brown hole as some sort of bridge from the past to the present?" said Zack's butt.

"It's possible," said Eleanor. "And not just *the* Great White Butt. *All* of the Great White Butts."

"But why?" said Zack. "Why doesn't he just stay there with all his pals where he belongs?"

"Ah," said Ned. "I think I can answer that one. If my — and Robobutt's — calculations are correct, that message was written just before a very important event in Earth's history. Less than twenty-four hours after that message was written, a giant arseteroid slammed into the Earth and caused the extinction of all the buttosaurs, including the Great White Butts."

"And my gran," said Zack, stunned.

"And your gran," said Ned.

CHAPTER SIXTEEN

Rewind

Zack felt dizzy as he tried to make sense of Ned's words.

"So, let me get this straight," said Eleanor, frowning. "The Great White Butt is actually a Great White Buttosaur, a relic from the times when Great White Buttosaurs ruled the Earth."

"Correct," said Ned.

"And in the original history of the Earth all of the Great White Buttosaurs — except for the Great White Butt — were wiped out when a giant arseteroid hit the earth."

"Correct again," said Ned.

"But now, the Great White Butt has taken advantage of the brown hole's closeness to Earth to provide an escape route from the doomed past to the safety of the present."

"Exactly," said Ned.

"So the answer is simple," said Eleanor.

"It is?" said Zack's butt.

"Yes," said Eleanor. "We have to go back in time and stop the Great White Butt from carrying out its evacuation."

"But how?" said Zack.

"I'll spell it out for you," said Eleanor. "We go back to the past. We use Robobutt's nuclear wart-head to terminate the Great White Butt once and for all. Without the Great White Butt's help, the other Great White Butts won't be able to return to the present. They'll die — as they did, and as they should have done — when the arseteroid hits. Meanwhile, we'll return to the present . . . a *Great White Butt-free* present."

Zack gulped as he realized what Eleanor was proposing. "But that's dangerous," he said.

"So is staying here, in case you hadn't noticed," said Eleanor.

"But brown holes are unpredictable," said Zack. "We went into the same brown hole as the rest of them and we didn't go back into the past. What makes you think that it will work this time?"

"There's a better . . ." started Ned, but he was cut off by Eleanor.

"Let me handle him," said Eleanor. "He's a bit slow."

"I am *not* slow!" said Zack.

"You are," said his butt.

"Thanks for your support," said Zack. "You're supposed to be on my side."

"On your backside to be exact," said his butt.

Zack ignored his butt and turned to Eleanor. "All I'm

saying is what your father told us, over and over. They are *too dangerous*. And besides, my mom made me *promise*."

Tears filled Eleanor's eyes. "Zack," she said slowly, "neither your mom nor my dad is alive anymore. Promises made back then don't count. Neither do warnings. That was another world ago. Things have changed, and we have to adapt or we could very well end up extinct ourselves."

Zack was silent.

"Besides," said Eleanor. "We owe it to their memory to try to stop this. It's what they would have wanted us to do, no matter how dangerous." She paused. "It's what they would do — if they could."

Zack looked at the sickening images on the screens.

He knew Eleanor was right, but he was still terrified.

"There is another way," said Ned.

"Another way?" said Eleanor. "What are you talking about?"

CHAPTER SEVENTEEN

Preparations

Well," said Ned, "apart from her other features, Robobutt is fully equipped for time travel."

"Why didn't you say so?" said Eleanor.

"I've been trying to," said Ned. "But you wouldn't let me."

"Time travel?" said Zack. "But don't you need a . . ."

"Perambulic merimbulator?" said Ned.

"Yes!" said Zack, who'd studied time machine technology for a school project.

"I've got one," said Ned. "Robobutt instructed me how to make a rudimentary one out of a tin can and an old mattress spring."

"Awesome!" said Zack. "And it can go all the way back? Sixty-five million years?"

"Yes," said Ned. "At least, I think so."

"What do you mean, you THINK so?" said Eleanor.

"Well," said Ned. "I've never actually tested it. I've

been too busy. But you know what they say about time travel. There's no time like the present!"

Zack rolled his eyes at Ned's joke.

"Well, what are we waiting for?" said Eleanor. "Let's do it!"

"Right you are," said Ned. "Robobutt . . . prepare for time travel!"

"Affirmative," said Robobutt. "Please enter the passenger pods and secure safety harnesses. I will then present a short film about time travel safety."

"Skip the safety presentation," said Ned. "We have to get out of here before we end up Buttageddonized ourselves. We've got a human race to save."

"Understood," said Robobutt. "Safety presentation suspended. But please exercise extreme caution at all times. Even the tiniest change to the past may have catastrophic effects on the future."

"Warning heard and understood," said Ned. He led Zack, Zack's butt, and Eleanor over to a bank of what looked like six glass coffins.

"Well, whatever we do," said Zack's butt as it lay down in one of the pods, "It can't be any worse than what's already happening."

"The small butt speaks the truth," said Robobutt.

CHAPTER EIGHTEEN

Countdown

"Time travel commencing in T-minus twenty seconds," announced Robobutt.

Zack took a deep breath as he climbed into his pod. His stomach was churning. They were about to voyage sixty-five million years into the past on the most important butt-fighting mission ever undertaken in the entire history of butt-fighting.

The world — as they'd known it — was doomed.

Buttageddon was nigh.

"Time travel commencing in T-minus fifteen seconds," announced Robobutt.

Zack looked at Ned, who was adjusting the dials on the temporal navigator — a domelike structure that allowed them to control both the direction and the distance of their passage through time.

"Time travel commencing in T-minus ten seconds," announced Robobutt.

45

At last Ned finished setting their course. He walked up to his pod, climbed inside, and strapped himself in. He signaled to Zack to do the same.

"Time travel commencing in T-minus five seconds," announced Robobutt. "Five . . ."

Zack fumbled with his belt.

"Four . . ."

"Stupid belt!" said Zack.

"Three . . ."

"Great!" he said. "Most important mission ever, and no safety belt!"

"Two . . ."

Zack clutched the handgrips on his pod as tightly as he could.

"One . . ."

Zack closed his eyes.

CHAPTER NINETEEN

650,000,000 B.C.

Zack held his breath and waited . . . but nothing seemed to happen. He opened his eyes. "When do we leave?" he said.

"We're already there!" said Ned, climbing out of his pod.

"What do you mean?" said Eleanor, sitting up. "It didn't feel like we moved at all."

"No," said Ned. "Technically speaking, we didn't move. Time moved through us."

"Huh?" said Eleanor, frowning.

"We must have moved *somewhere*," said Zack, standing in front of the buttcam monitors. "Look!"

Eleanor, Ned, and Zack's butt came over and joined Zack at the screens.

Buttcam now consisted of a single supersized image provided by a hidden camera mounted on the top of Robobutt.

They were looking at a small inlet with a range of rocky, treeless mountains in the distance. Robobutt was sitting in the middle of a large stretch of featureless mudflats.

Apart from a strong wind that buffeted Robobutt's riveted steel panels, there was nothing but mudflats and water and smoking buttcanoes for as far as they could see.

There was no sign of life.

No animals.

No people.

No butts.

Nothing.

"Where are we?" said Zack's butt.

"I don't know," said Eleanor, "but if this is sixty-five million B.C., where are all the buttosaurs? There's not a lot of action out there."

"No," said Ned, looking a little worried as he bent over his temporal navigator. "I think I might have made a slight miscalculation."

"How much of a slight miscalculation?" said Eleanor.

"Well," said Ned, "instead of going back sixty-five million years, we've gone back *six hundred fifty* million years."

CHAPTER TWENTY

Mud

Six hundred fifty million years!" spluttered Eleanor. "That is not a slight miscalculation, Ned. That is a miscalculation of major proportions!"

"It's only an extra zero," said Ned.

"That extra zero makes a big difference!" said Eleanor. "Five hundred eighty-five million years' worth of difference, to be exact."

"I told you Robobutt's time travel capabilities hadn't been tested," said Ned, sheepishly. "There must be a loose screw in the temporal navigator."

"I think I know where the loose screw is," said Eleanor. "It's . . ."

"Take it easy, Eleanor," said Zack. "I'm sure Ned's doing his best."

"Well this is just great, isn't it?" said Eleanor. "While Ned tinkers with his time travel toy, the Earth is being

Buttageddonized and we're five hundred eighty-five million years from being able to do anything about it."

"That's not technically correct," said Zack. "Earth isn't in any immediate danger of Buttageddon. . . . it's not going to happen for another six hundred fifty million years. Ned's got plenty of time to figure it out."

"Oh, well, that's all right then," said Eleanor. "In the meantime we might just as well relax and take a vacation. Anyone up for a swim?"

"I wouldn't do that if I were you," said Zack's butt, who had been busy gazing at the screen all this time. "There's something moving out there."

"Impossible," said Robobutt. "Oxygen levels are too low to sustain advanced life forms."

"But there's something moving!" insisted Zack's butt. "Look, there, just at the water's edge."

"Move in for a closer look, Robobutt," said Ned.

With a barely audible sigh, Robobutt slowly moved forward. As she did so, the butt-fighters were amazed to see movement in the mud. There was a small shape wriggling on the surface.

"That's close enough, Robobutt," said Ned. "Whatever it is, we don't want to alarm it."

"I hate to say I told you so," said Zack's butt, "but I told you so."

"I stand corrected," said Robobutt. "We are witnessing one of the earliest, most primitive forms of life on the planet."

"What is it?" said Zack.

"I do not know," said Robobutt. "Insufficient data."

"We can fix that," said Eleanor. In an instant she had

been transformed from a frustrated butt-fighter into an eager scientist. She grabbed one of the extravehicular butt-fighting suits hanging up next to the teleportation tube.

"What are you doing, Eleanor?" said Zack.

"You heard Robobutt," said Eleanor. "She needs data. I'm going out to take a closer look. Six hundred fifty million years takes us right into the heart of the geological period known as the Precambrian Era. There are not a whole lot of fossils dating back this far — and it's not like we'll be back this way again. It's too good an opportunity to miss. The more data that Robobutt — and we — have, the better our chances of success."

"If you survive long enough to gather the data, that is," said Ned. "I wouldn't leave the ship if I were you."

"Yeah?" said Eleanor. "Well, you're not me, Ned. Besides, how dangerous can it be out there? It's got to be a lot safer than where we just came from."

"Guess I'd better come with you, then," sighed Zack. He knew it was no use arguing with Eleanor.

"Which means I'll have to come to look after you both," said Zack's butt.

Zack smiled. "Thanks," he said. "I knew I could count on you. Ned?"

Ned was already climbing into his suit. "If you think I'm going to let you crazy kids go out there on your own, you need your heads examined. Robobutt — you're in charge. If there's any sign of trouble I want you to beam us up straight away."

"Affirmative," said Robobutt.

CHAPTER TWENTY-ONE

Buttolution

A strong wind greeted the butt-fighters as they teleported onto the gray sludge of prehistoric Earth. They leaned into the squall and began squelching across the ancient mudflats.

"Can I ride on your shoulder, Zack?" said his butt. "I'm tired."

"But we've only just started," said Zack. "How can you be tired?"

"My legs aren't as big — or as strong — as yours," it said.

"Okay," said Zack, bending down. "Climb aboard."

"It's amazing," said Eleanor. "The whole Earth. All new. Completely unspoiled."

"I wouldn't be so sure of that," said Ned.

"Why?" said Zack.

"Our friend in the mud, there," said Ned, pointing.

"See the little crease running from top to bottom? If I didn't know better, I'd say it was a . . . butt."

As they closed in on it, Eleanor put out her arm to stop Zack and Ned. "Slow and quiet," she said. "Let's not disturb it unnecessarily. It doesn't look dangerous, but you never know."

They nodded and moved the last few feet toward the primitive life form in silence.

At first glance Zack thought it was a jellyfish. Then, when he looked closer, it appeared to be *two* jellyfish, but without tentacles, just four stumpy little protuberances. And then, like a magic 3-D picture coming into focus, the two jellyfish globes merged into one single organism and Zack realized what he was actually looking at. The two halves were joined with a crevice running through the middle. Ned was right. It was a butt. Primitive and barely formed, but unmistakably a butt.

Eleanor let out a long breath. "So, Sir Roger Francis Rectum was right," she said.

"About what?" said Zack.

"Buttolution!" she said. "His theory was that the first life forms were butts. Look — you can see the little stumps that will one day be arms and legs. Sir Roger was ridiculed for his beliefs by the scientific community of his time, but he was right. We evolved from butts, Zack."

"I like that theory!" said Zack's butt.

"It's not a theory anymore," said Eleanor. "It's now an official fact. At least it will be once I've taken a photograph."

"I wouldn't do that if I were you," said Ned. "The flash might disturb it."

"I don't think so," said Eleanor. "A life form this primitive won't have any visual receptors. They don't evolve for at least another hundred million years."

Before Ned could stop her, Eleanor took a small camera out of her pocket and took a photo, bathing the primeval butt in a momentary flash of bright white light.

CHAPTER TWENTY-TWO

Hatch

The reaction was instant.

The butt flipped up and over onto its back, its stumps wiggling crazily.

"Stand back!" said Ned. "It may not have an eye, but it's got heat sensors."

The butt-fighters gave the butt a wide berth as it continued its agonized flipping. But as it flipped, it revealed that it was protecting a small clutch of white eggs. And whether it was due to the flipping of the butt or the heat of the camera's flash, or whether it was just the right time to do so, they were beginning to hatch.

The butt-fighters stood and watched in wonder as dozens of the eggs cracked open and a clutch of tiny jellylike butts emerged. All except one, which, unlike its brothers and sisters, was not see-through jelly, but a pure, gleaming white.

"Look at that!" said Zack. "It's a mutant!"

Eleanor clutched his arm. "It's *white*, Zack," she said. "Do you realize what we're looking at?"

"Yes," said Zack, "a mutant. That's how buttolution works, isn't it? Little mutations to the basic patterns that give an organism an advantage — or a disadvantage, as the case may be."

"Definitely a disadvantage in this case," said Ned.

"I don't understand," said Zack.

"Gee, you can be dense, Zack," said Eleanor. "*It's the Great White Butt!*"

"I think that's jumping to conclusions, isn't it?" said Zack. "Out of all the primeval mudflats in all the possible years that we could have landed in, we touch down right in the exact spot at the exact time that the Great White Butt is being hatched? You've got to be joking!"

But a glance at the terrified faces of his companions told Zack that he was in the minority on this one.

"Stranger things have happened," said Eleanor.

Not many, thought Zack, as he stared at the small white butt. And then an idea began to form in his mind.

An idea so huge that he could hardly contain it in his head.

An idea so daring that only one butt-fighter on the planet could possibly have conceived it, let alone considered it.

What if, he thought, what if I killed the Great White Butt right now? Killed it in the nest. Killed it before it had a chance to grow up and do all the evil that it was going to do. There would be no enormous buttcanoes capable of gassing the entire world. No zombie butt invasions.

And, most important of all, no Buttageddon.

Of course, there would be no such thing as butt-fighters, either, but Zack realized this was not about him.

This was bigger than all of them.

This was about the future of the entire world.

Hadn't the Blind Butt-feeler predicted this?

Hadn't she told him that he would be the savior of free men everywhere . . . past, present, and future?

To what else, apart from this moment, could she possibly have been referring?

Zack put his butt down on the ground. He drew his butt-gun from his butt-fighting utility belt and raised it to his shoulder.

CHAPTER TWENTY-THREE

Exterminate!

Z ack!" yelled Eleanor. "What do you think you're doing?"

"We have to kill it," said Zack.

"No!" said Ned.

"What do you mean, 'no'?" said Zack. "One shot now could prevent a lot of suffering and save millions of lives in the future. It's the Great White Butt. Or at least its father. Or its father's father."

"Or its father's father's father," said Zack's butt helpfully.

"Whatever," said Zack. "I have to kill it. Now. While there's still time."

"But it hasn't done anything wrong," said Ned. "Not yet. You would be killing an innocent butt."

"But it's not going to *stay* innocent!" said Zack. "We *know* that! That's why we're here!"

"No," said Ned. "That's *not* why we're here. We came

back for one reason and one reason only: to prevent the Great White Butt from sending prehistoric Great White Butts into the future and upsetting the natural buttolution of the planet. We didn't come to strip it — or any other carbon-based life-form — of its right to life. I don't like the idea of butt rebellion or buttcanoes or zombie butts any more than you do, but if we kill it now we'll be no better than the Great White Butt himself."

"Great White Butts killed my parents, Ned," said Zack. "Great White Butts killed your parents, Eleanor. And they destroyed our planet. Doesn't that count for anything?"

"Of course it does, Zack," said Ned. "But it doesn't change the fact that this is not our decision to make."

"If it's not ours then whose is it?" said Zack.

"Nobody's!" said Ned. "It's too big a change. Sure, you might get rid of the Great White Butt, but there's no telling what else you might change — or create — in the process. You might create the conditions for the emergence of a monster that makes the Great White Butt look as harmless as a pussycat! Don't try to play God, Zack."

"I never said I was God," said Zack. "I'm just a butt-fighter and I've got a butt to fight."

"I agree with Ned," said Eleanor. "I don't like the Great White Butt any more than you do, but two wrongs don't make a right."

"True," said Zack. "But a stitch in time saves nine. How many more people have to die? How many more planets have to be destroyed before we take action?"

"That's enough," said Ned. "I order you to put down your gun immediately, Zack. I can see why you want to do what you want to do, but you could be introducing catastrophic time travel errors that I cannot allow myself — or any of us — to be responsible for."

Zack was silent.

"Zack?" said Ned. "Did you hear me? I gave you a direct order!"

"I'm sorry, Ned," said Zack. "I cannot obey that order."

"Fine," said Ned, lunging toward Zack. "Then I'll obey it for you!"

Zack watched Ned as he sailed toward him, as if in slow motion.

Ned's heavy body knocked Zack sideways.

But not before Zack's shaking finger had squeezed the butt-gun trigger.

As Zack fell, a volley of butt-gun bullets sprayed the nest. The newly hatched butts — at least, the ones that weren't hit by the bullets — scattered like a flock of startled birds.

"You idiot, Zack!" yelled Eleanor. "Now look what you've done!"

Zack ignored Eleanor, jumped to his feet, and kept shooting until all the butts lay dead in the mud.

Well, *almost* all of them. All except for the white one.

"Zack!" said his butt. "It's still alive!"

"Where is it?" yelled Zack. "Where did it go?"

"Over there!" said his butt, pointing.

Zack turned.

The mutant hatchling had already moved just out of range.

Zack squelched through the slime after it, shooting all the while.

But it was fast.

And agile.

Zack's bullets hit the mud and the water around the butt as it rolled first one way and then the other.

As much as Zack hated the Great White Butt, he had to admire it. Even at this early age it was already clearly a survivor.

And even as he had this thought, the hatchling flew into the air and took off into the sky.

Whether it was the first time in the history of the Earth that a butt had left the safety of the mud and taken to the air, Zack had no way of knowing. But he wasn't about to let it get away.

"Robobutt!" Zack yelled at the top of his voice. "Hurry!"

CHAPTER TWENTY-FOUR

Butt Hunt

But Robobutt was already in the air.

Even before Zack had finished speaking he was engulfed by Robobutt's matter-transporting beam. In an instant he found himself sprawled on the control room floor along with Ned, Eleanor, and his butt.

"Follow that butt!" said Zack, picking himself up and rushing to the viewing screens.

"Affirmative," said Robobutt. "Tracking system locked on. Hold tight."

Zack grabbed the temporal navigator to keep from falling backward as Robobutt shot up into the air.

The sky was beginning to turn from blue to black as Robobutt flew higher and higher in pursuit.

"Ned!" said Eleanor. "We're leaving the atmosphere!"

"Don't worry," said Ned. "Robobutt is space-travel

ready and full of stinkant juice. We can go anywhere. But I'm not sure this is such a good idea."

"We've got to finish what we started," said Zack.

"What *you* started," said Eleanor.

"Maybe we should just let it go," said Zack's butt.

"No," said Zack, his eyes burning. "We have to do whatever it takes. Go wherever we need to go. This is the most important butt hunt in history! If we can catch this butt, there won't be any need for anyone to catch a butt ever again. Without the Great White Butt inciting butts to rebellion, butts across the univarse will be able to work *with* their bodies instead of against them."

"But *I* work with you," said Zack's butt.

"*Now* you do," said Zack. "But it hasn't always been that way, has it?"

Before Zack's butt could reply, Robobutt suddenly turned steeply.

"Changing course," said Robobutt.

"Ouch!" said Zack as he lost his grip on the navigator and fell face first against the buttcam screens. The other butt-fighters fell right on top of him, powerless to resist the intense B-forces unleashed by the dive. Zack could see that the tiny white butt was now heading back toward the ground. But not for long.

Zack was close to blacking out when Robobutt changed course again. This time the butt-fighters fell hard against the back wall.

Then Robobutt changed course again.

And again.

And yet again.

The butt-fighters were being thrown around like dirty socks in a washing machine.

Zack felt his head smash against something hard.

There was a huge crash.

And then silence.

CHAPTER TWENTY-FIVE

65,000,000 BC

Ouch!" said Robobutt. "That hurt!"

Inside Robobutt, her hapless occupants lay on the floor and blinked stupidly at one another.

They tried to remember who they were.

They tried to remember where they were.

They tried to remember why they were where they were.

Zack's butt was the first to fully reorient itself.

"Zack!" it said, jumping onto his lap. "Wake up!"

Zack looked at his butt dumbly.

"Pleased to meet you," he said, extending his hand. "My name is Zack."

"I know who you are!" said his butt, slapping Zack's hand away. "It's me — your butt — remember?"

Zack tried to focus on the small pink excitable butt in front of him. It looked familiar, but he was having a lot of trouble remembering why.

"You look like somebody I know . . ." said Zack.

"Maybe this will jog your memory," said his butt, huffing in Zack's face.

The obnoxious odor sent Zack into a doubled-over coughing fit, but when he'd come to, he remembered exactly who he was. And exactly who *it* was.

"Why, you . . ." he said to his butt, reaching out to strangle it.

"Steady, Zack," it said, jumping out of the way. "You were delirious. I had to do it. I'm sorry."

"Not as sorry as I am," said Zack, stifling another coughing fit. Beside him, Eleanor and Ned were coughing and returning to their senses as well.

Zack rose to his feet — a little dizzy from both the bad air and the blow to his head. He staggered to the buttcam screens.

He could see that they were in a lush cocobutt-tree forest. The cocobutt-trees were enormous — taller than any he had ever seen — their thick brown fronds blocking out the sky.

"I don't believe it," said Ned from behind him. "I don't believe it!"

"What?" said Zack.

Ned was bent over the temporal navigator. "I don't know how this has happened, but the temporal navigator indicates that we are deep in the heart of the late Cretaceous period."

"What does that mean?" said Zack's butt.

"It's sixty-five million years BC," said Ned, still shaking his head in wonder.

"You mean we just traveled through time?" said Eleanor. "Forward?"

"It would seem so," said Ned, scratching his beard. "It appears that we're exactly where we need to be."

"Thanks, Ned!" said Eleanor. "You're a genius!"

"I didn't do anything," said Ned. "Thank Robobutt!"

"Thanks, Robobutt," said Eleanor.

"I cannot take credit for this outcome," said Robobutt. "Thank Zack."

"Me?" said Zack, rubbing his head. "What did I do?"

"When you fell, your head hit the temporal navigator control panel," said Robobutt. "The force not only initiated time travel, but at the same time fixed the loose screw that caused the five-hundred-eighty-five-million-year error on our last trip."

"I did all that?" said Zack, proudly.

"It was the *least* you could do," said Eleanor.

"What do you mean?" said Zack.

"You know exactly what I mean," said Eleanor. "It was the least you could do to make up for the botched attempt to kill the Great White Butt."

"At least I tried," said Zack. "Better to try and fail than never to have tried at all."

"No," said Eleanor. "Not in this case. In this case it was better *not* to try than to fail. You just made an enemy of the Great White Butt."

"What are you talking about?" said Zack. "He wasn't exactly our friend to begin with!"

"No," she said. "Because you tried to kill him."

"You've been trying to kill him for a lot longer than I have," said Zack.

"Oh, really?" said Eleanor. "I seem to remember that it was *you* who fired the first ever shot at him."

"Huh?" said Zack.

"Five hundred and eighty-five million years ago," said Eleanor. "And if my memory serves me correctly, I also seem to remember that you *missed*."

"Ned dived on me," said Zack.

"I was just trying to stop you from creating a bigger problem than we already had," said Ned.

"What could be bigger than Buttageddon?" said Zack.

"Buttageddon didn't exist at that moment," said Ned. "You were way out of line and way off mission. You might have killed the Great White Butt, yes, but by doing so, you might also have completely altered the course of buttolution and erased the possibility of humans even evolving."

"Would that have been such a bad thing?" said Zack's butt.

The butt-fighters all turned and glared at Zack's butt.

"Just kidding," it said quickly.

"I was only trying to do what I thought was best," said Zack quietly.

"Yeah, well, no more heroics," said Eleanor. "You might have a certificate and a medal, but butt-fighting is a team effort, and the sooner you realize that, the better."

Zack nodded dejectedly.

Maybe she was right.

Suddenly the silence of the forest was broken by a horrendous howl. The ground began to shake around them.

"What's that?" said Zack's butt, as the howl sounded again, even closer this time.

"I don't know," said Zack. "But whatever it is, it sounds like it's in pain."

"Robobutt!" said Ned. "Can you identify what is making that sound?"

"Insufficient data," said Robobutt.

Ned stood up and began rifling through a collection of books on an overhead shelf. He selected a thick volume called *What Buttosaur Is That?* and began quickly leafing through the pages. "Uh-oh," he said. "If I didn't know better I'd say that's the sound of a tyrannosore-arse. . . ."

"And here it is!" said Eleanor, as the image of an enormous, throbbing red butt, its cheeks lined with two rows of huge, sharp, daggerlike teeth, appeared on the screens and began charging toward them.

CHAPTER TWENTY-SIX

Tyrannosore-arse

Zack stared at the buttcam screens. He had seen some terrifying and unpleasant sights in his short career as a butt-fighter, but few as terrifying — or as unpleasant — as this.

"What are you waiting for, Ned?" said Eleanor. "Get this hunk of tin moving!"

"Robobutt is not a hunk of tin," said Robobbutt. "I am Robobutt. Fully riveted reinforced steel cheeks. Turbo-assisted jet repulsion units. Nuclear wart-head equipped. Matter transport assisted entry and exit. Inside and outside voice options. Onboard tea- and coffee-making facilities. And I am self-wiping!"

"Spare us the details," said Eleanor. "Just run!"

"Unable to run," said Robobutt. "Currently perform-ing damage assessment."

"No time for that now!" said Ned. "Move!"

But it was already too late.

Zack stared, transfixed and sickened, as the tyrannosore-arse cheek-butted Robobutt and sent her flying through the cocobutt-tree forest.

Zack, Eleanor, Ned, and Zack's butt were thrown violently from one side of Robobutt to the other. They landed heavily on top of each other as Robobutt came to rest wedged between two cocobutt-trees.

"Do you think it's finished with us?" said Zack.

There was another howl and then the ground started to shake again.

"I suspect it's only just begun," said Ned, looking up from his guidebook. "It says here that the tyrannosore-arse likes to play with its food . . . before eating it."

Through the upside-down buttcam of Robobutt, they could see the tyrannosore-arse crashing toward them again.

"If this is playing, then I'd hate to see it when it gets serious," said Zack's butt.

"Me too," said Eleanor. "Switch to manual control, Ned."

"Good idea," said Ned.

"Bad idea!" said Robobutt. "Strongly recom —"

Robobutt's voice was shut off midsentence as Ned pulled down on a lever.

"Done," said Ned.

"Then what are we waiting for?" said Eleanor. "Go!"

"I'm trying," said Ned, "but we're wedged between the trees!"

"Hurry!" said Zack, watching as the enraged

tyrannosore-arse opened its cheeks again and clamped them down hard over the top of Robobutt.

Everything went dark for a second, and then they felt Robobutt being lifted free of the trees.

"It's got us!" said Ned.

Suddenly the room was filled with light as the tyrannosore-arse hurled Robobutt through the air once more.

This time, however, Ned was able to activate Robobutt's "flight" program, and they hit the forest floor running.

"Good going, Ned," said Eleanor as Robobutt dodged cocobutt-trees and leaped over rivers and bogs.

"It's still chasing us!" said Zack, listening to the loud, outraged howls close behind them.

"Relax!" said Ned. "This is just a walk in the park for Robobutt. Wait till I really get this baby going."

"I wouldn't do that if I were you," said Eleanor, placing her hand on Ned's to stop him from opening the throttle.

"Why not?" he said.

"Look," said Eleanor, her eyes wide.

CHAPTER TWENTY-SEVEN

Run!

Directly in front of Robobutt was another tyrannosore-arse, even bigger than the one chasing them. And not only was it bigger, it was redder. And louder. It pawed the forest floor angrily, howled, and charged toward them.

Ned didn't hesitate.

He pushed the emergency stop button, sending them all piling toward the buttcam screens.

"What do we do now?" said Eleanor.

"I don't know," said Ned.

"Ned, I think it's time to put Robobutt back in control of herself," said Zack. "Maybe she will have had time to figure out what to do."

"Can't hurt," said Ned, throwing the switch back to automatic.

"Hello, I am Robobutt," said Robobutt, crackling back to life. "Fully riveted reinforced steel cheeks.

Turbo-assisted jet repulsion units. Nuclear wart-head equipped. Matter transport assisted entry and exit. Inside and outside voice options. Onboard tea- and coffee-making facilities. And I am self-wiping!"

"Robobutt!" said Ned. "I know! I built you, remember? It's Ned! Ned Smelly!"

"I know who you are," said Robobutt. "You turned me off. Don't do that again."

"Sorry," said Ned. "But you've got to help us. We're being attacked by two tyrannosore-arses. What should we do?"

"Leave them to me," announced Robobutt. "Meanwhile, I advise you to abandon ship immediately! It's going to get rough. Too rough for passengers. I'll pick you up later."

Zack, Ned, Eleanor, and Zack's butt didn't argue. They assembled in the teleportation tube and beamed themselves clear of Robobutt only moments before the two tyrannosore-arses closed in.

"Ned!" said Robobutt, in her loudest outside voice. "You forgot this!"

Robobutt beamed Ned's copy of *What Buttosaur Is That?* into his hand.

"Thanks, Robobutt!" cried Ned. "Be careful!"

"Do not concern yourself about me," she said. "I am Robobutt. Fully riveted reinforced steel cheeks. Turbo-assisted jet repulsion units. Nuclear wart-head equipped. Matter transport assisted entry and exit. Inside and outside voice options. Onboard tea- and coffee-making facilities. And I am self-wiping! I am perfectly capable of handling myself."

"Come on, Ned," said Eleanor, trying to drag him away from Robobutt.

"But they're going to destroy her!" said Ned. "My baby!"

"They'll destroy us if we don't find a place to hide," said Eleanor, grabbing Ned and dragging him into the thick undergrowth.

CHAPTER TWENTY-EIGHT

Tricerabutt

The butt-fighters fought their way through the shaded semitropical undergrowth. Zack wiped his sweating brow and marveled at the difference that five hundred eighty-five million years can make. The Earth had come alive. There were cocobutt-tree forests in place of gray sludge. Giant mutant blowflies droned around their heads. Enormous red stinkants lumbered in single file across the forest floor. And, of course, terrifying buttosaurs ruled the planet.

As they hacked against thick vines and even thicker spider webs, the butt-fighters could hear Robobutt preparing to do battle with the tyrannosore-arses.

"I must warn you," said Robobutt, "I have fully riveted reinforced steel cheeks. Turbo-assisted jet repulsion units . . ."

There was a loud tyrannosore-arse howl.

A sickening metallic crunch.

And then . . . silence.

Zack glanced back at Ned.

Ned looked at Zack.

"Nuclear wart-head equipped," said a voice. "Matter transport assisted entry and exit. Inside and outside voice options. Onboard tea- and coffee-making . . ."

The butt-fighters grinned with relief. But not for long.

There was another howl.

Followed by another crunch.

Silence.

And then . . .

". . . and I am self-wiping!"

A third crunch.

And a fourth.

And a fifth.

Ned put his hands over his ears. "Robobutt!" he cried. "My Robobutt!"

"Come on, Ned," said Eleanor, putting her arm around his shoulders. "We have to look after ourselves now. It's what Robobutt would want."

Zack, who was leading, pushed his way into a rectangular clearing that was about the size of a soccer field.

"Hey!" said his butt, trying to brighten the mood. "Anyone for soccer?"

"We don't have a ball," said Ned.

"We could use Zack's butt," said Eleanor.

"Not funny!" said Zack's butt.

They were halfway across the clearing when Zack screamed.

"Shut up!" said Eleanor. "Do you want the tyrannosore-arses to hear us?"

"No," said Zack. "But . . ."

"But what?" said Eleanor.

Zack was speechless.

He could only point.

Charging toward them was a huge armored butt with three cheeks. Each cheek had a large wart in its center.

And each wart was sharpened to a deadly point.

"Oh no," said Ned, looking from his fieldguide to the buttosaur and then back to the book. "A tricerabutt!"

"We can see that!" said Zack's butt. "How do you stop it?"

"You can't," said Ned, consulting his book. "It says here that nothing can stop a charging tricerabutt."

They all stared helplessly at the triple-cheeked beast as it lumbered toward them, picking up speed as it came.

Zack gulped.

In the space of a single morning they'd been giant-brown-blobbified, traveled millions of years into the past, been involved in a wild butt chase, traveled millions of years into the future, and been attacked by not one, but *two* tyrannosore-arses. They needed a tricerabutt attack like they needed a hole in the head . . . or *three* holes, as was a very real possibility in this situation.

"Gee," said Zack. "The Cretaceous is a really fun place. We should come here more often."

"We'll be lucky to get out alive," said Eleanor.

The tricerabutt snorted as it ran.

The stink made Zack feel faint.

The butt-fighters were in trouble.

Big trouble.

Bad trouble.

Triple trouble.

They didn't have time to run back to where they'd come from. The jungle was too dense. And running forward was out of the question.

Then Zack had an idea.

"Stand back, everyone," he said.

"What are you going to do?" said Zack's butt, backing away with Ned and Eleanor.

Zack pulled what was left of his butt-fighter's certificate out of his butt-fighting belt and, using the two top corners, held it out to his side, matador-style.

"Be careful, Zack!" said his butt.

"'Careful' is my middle name," said Zack.

"No, it's not," said his butt. "It's Henry!"

"Shut up!" said Zack.

Zack Henry Freeman took a deep breath and focused. "You want a piece of me?" he said to the charging tricerabutt. "Come and get it!"

CHAPTER TWENTY-NINE

Olé!

The tricerabutt needed no encouragement.

It was already halfway across the clearing.

Zack had barely fluttered the sheet of paper in his hand and stepped nimbly to one side before the triple-cheeked brute charged past him, snorting great clouds of methane.

"Bravo!" yelled Zack's butt.

"Olé!" said Zack, feeling slightly dizzy from the double dose of noxious fumes issuing forth from between the tricerabutt's three cheeks.

The tricerabutt smashed uselessly into the under-growth at the other end of the clearing. It pulled itself out, turned to face Zack, and began charging again.

"Olé, again!" said Zack, jumping out of the way at the last moment as the beast charged past him.

"Good going, Zack," said Eleanor.

But Zack was not feeling well. He was desperately

trying to fight the methane fog that was starting to cloud his thinking.

The tricerabutt turned once again and lowered its cheeks so that its three deadly warts were pointing directly at Zack.

It pawed the ground and began its run.

Zack tried to concentrate. With great difficulty. To his alarm he saw not one, but *three* separate tricerabutts coming at him. He waved his certificate first at one, then the other, and then the third.

"Zack!" yelled his butt, who had figured out that Zack was suffering methane-induced triple vision. "Close one eye!"

But, although this was excellent advice, Zack was too far gone to understand — or even to hear — what his butt was saying to him. He doubled over in a violent coughing fit.

"Zack!" yelled his butt. "Get up! It's coming!"

But Zack was coughing too hard to hear his butt's warning. Or the thundering of the tricerabutt's hooves.

Zack's butt ran to Zack and tried to pull him out of the way. But Zack, now on his knees, was too heavy for the small butt to move.

The tricerabutt, sensing a kill, lowered its mighty wart-horns close to the ground as it closed in on its helpless quarry.

"Leave me," spluttered Zack. "Save yourself while there's still time!"

"Not on your life!" said his butt, taking the certificate from Zack's hand. "It's one for all and all for one! Got a match?"

CHAPTER THIRTY

Fire

Zack's butt jumped on top of Zack, pulled a match from his butt-fighting belt, and lit one corner of the certificate.

"Hey!" protested Zack. "That's my certificate!"

"It's mine, too!" said his butt, waving the certificate at the tricerabutt, which, despite its superior size and wart-horn power, screeched in terror at the sight of the naked flame.

The tricerabutt was running too fast to stop, however, and the best it could do was to swerve — a move which sent it sliding head first toward the trunk of a particularly thick cocobutt-tree.

WHAM!

It hit the tree with such force that all three of its wart-horns lodged deeply into the trunk.

Zack's butt screamed in pain and dropped the burning paper.

Zack quickly stomped on the flames and put what was left of the certificate back into his belt.

He looked at the tricerabutt. It was scraping the ground with its foot, snorting, and desperately trying to pull its wart-horns out of the tree.

"Well done!" Zack said to his butt.

"Always happy to help," said Zack's butt. "Now, let's get out of here!"

"With pleasure," said Zack, scooping up his butt and running to catch up with Eleanor and Ned, who were at the edge of the clearing trying to find a way into the dense undergrowth.

"This is hopeless," said Eleanor, pushing against a thick curtain of vines. "There's no way in."

"*Psst!*" said a voice a few feet away. "In here!"

Eleanor looked at Zack. "Did you say something?" she said.

"No," said Zack. "I thought you did."

"It wasn't me," said Eleanor, turning to Ned. "Was it you?"

"Not me," said Ned. "I thought it was Zack's butt."

"Nope," said Zack's butt, pointing to a tangled thicket of butt creeper. "It came from in there. Whoever — or whatever — it is, I think it wants us to go in."

"Well, what are we waiting for?" said Eleanor. "Anything's gotta be better than staying here."

"I don't know," said Ned. "Seems kind of risky." But at that moment the tricerabutt succeeded in pulling its horns out of the tree trunk. It turned on the helpless butt-fighters and, seeing they were without flame, began another charge. "Then, again," said Ned, "maybe it's worth a shot."

They hacked their way in.

Just in time.

Zack felt the tip of one of the tricerabutt's sharp warts brush his foot as he scrambled into the jungle's undergrowth behind the others.

CHAPTER THIRTY-ONE

Rescued

Zack pushed his way through the undergrowth into an old, hollow cocobutt-tree log.

It was dark and wet and mushy. He could feel the moisture seeping through his clothes. But at least it was safe.

And it was definitely a lot better than being torn to pieces by tyrannosore-arses or skewered on the end of a tricerabutt's horn.

As Zack's eyes adjusted to the darkness he saw a small butt, not unlike his own, standing in front of him. It looked like it had been living rough. Its dirty skin was caked in mud, scratches, and scars.

"You idiots!" the butt said. "What were you doing out there? This is a dangerous place!"

"We know," said Zack. "But we didn't have much choice. Our craft was attacked by tyrannosore-arses. We had to make a run for it."

"You have a craft?" said the butt, brightly. "One that could take us out of here?"

"We *had* a craft," said Eleanor. "We're not sure if we still do. She wasn't doing too well last time we saw her."

"Oh," said the butt, its cheeks sagging with obvious disappointment. "Never mind. It's good to have your company at least. Even if you were stupid enough to come to this awful place."

"We're not stupid," said Zack's butt, eyeing the new butt suspiciously. "And we're not idiots, either."

"Then what are you doing here?" said the butt.

"What are *you* doing here? That's the question," said Zack's butt.

"It wasn't my choice," said the butt. "I'll tell you that much! I was sucked into a brown hole."

"You mean you're not a buttosaur?" said Zack's butt.

The small butt was taken aback. "That's the kind of dumb question I'd expect from a *head*. Do I *look* like a buttosaur?" it demanded.

"Um, no, not really," said Zack's butt. "I guess I just thought . . ."

"Well, you thought wrong," said the butt. "Buttosaurs are big, dumb, and ugly. I, on the other hand, am small, smart, and if I do say so myself, quite cute."

"And very argumentative," said Zack's butt. "Don't forget that."

"You started it," said the butt.

"No, I didn't," said Zack's butt.

"You asked a stupid question," said the butt.

"I didn't think it was *that* stupid," said Zack's butt.

"And, besides, that's not the same as starting an argument."

"As good as," said the butt.

"No, it isn't!" said Zack's butt.

"Is too!" said the butt.

"Is not!" said Zack's butt.

"Stop it, both of you!" said Eleanor. "We've got more important things to do than to listen to your squabbling." She turned to the small butt. "Look," she said. "I don't know who you are or where you're from — we can deal with that later — but right now we are on a very important mission and you have to help us."

"I've already helped you," said the butt huffily. "And I think I'm beginning to regret it."

"Sorry," said Eleanor. "I'm a bit on edge. It's been a busy day."

"You're telling me," said the butt. "I was woken first thing by an enormous explosion. I went to investigate and would you believe it? It was a Great White Buttosaur! Just fell out of the sky!"

"You saw the Great White Butt?" said Zack.

"I saw *a* Great White Buttosaur," said the butt.

"Was anybody else with it?" said Eleanor.

"Not that I saw," said the butt. "No 'body,' anyway. But there have been an awful lot of blowflies around this morning. Big ones, too. Disgusting things. Flying around vomiting over everything."

"We've noticed," said Eleanor. "Where's the Great White Buttosaur now?"

The butt shrugged. "I don't know. On its way to the Crack of Doom, I guess."

"The Crack of Doom?" said Eleanor.

"Yes," said the butt. "It's where the Great White Buttosaurs breed. I expect it will be looking for its own kind. It's no fun being alone, you know."

As they talked they could hear the tricerabutt snuffling around, hunting for them. In the distance the tyrannosore-arses screeched and hooted. The drone of giant mutant zombie blowflies filled the late afternoon air.

"How far away is this Crack of Doom?" said Eleanor.

"It's about three hours north of here," said the butt.

"Can you take us there?" said Eleanor.

"I could," said the butt, "but you don't want to go there."

"Yes, we do," said Zack's butt.

"No, you don't," said the butt.

"Do!" said Zack's butt.

"Don't!" said the butt.

"Knock it off," said Zack to his butt. "You're not helping."

"I didn't start it," said Zack's butt.

"Yes, you did!" said the butt.

"No, I didn't!" said Zack's butt.

"Will you take us there or not?" said Eleanor loudly.

"You've got to be joking!" said the butt. "It's unbelievably dangerous. There are buttcanoes, giant stinkants, stinkbogs, chasms, and every type of buttosaur you can imagine between here and the Crack of Doom."

"How soon can we start?" said Eleanor. "We're in kind of a hurry."

CHAPTER THIRTY-TWO

Desperate

But you don't seem to understand," said the butt nervously. "Not even the most desperate of fools would undertake such a dangerous journey with so little chance of success."

"We *are* desperate," said Zack. "The Great White Butt is planning to send all the Great White Buttosaurs into the future, where they will completely destroy the Earth. We've already seen the results. Total destruction. Of everything. Buttageddon!"

"Buttageddon?" whispered the butt.

CHAPTER THIRTY-THREE

Buttageddon!!!

Buttageddon," said Eleanor, nodding.

"Buttageddon," said Ned.

"Buttageddon," said Zack's butt.

"Buttageddon," said Zack. "And you are our only hope of stopping it."

The butt nodded solemnly. "I understand," it said. "If that's the case, and you're sure that's where you need to go, then I'll be your guide. But you have to do exactly as I say, agreed?"

The butt-fighters all nodded.

All the butt-fighters, that is, except for Zack's butt.

Zack prodded it.

"Okay," it mumbled reluctantly.

CHAPTER THIRTY-FOUR

Suspicion

They set off with the small butt leading the way and Zack's butt bringing up the rear.

The harsh sounds — and horrible smells — of strange buttosaurs filled the air. As they walked, Zack used a large branch to swat away a giant mutant zombie blowfly that was circling his head.

"Hurry up," said Zack to his butt. "I don't want to get too far behind."

"I *am* hurrying," said his butt.

The giant mutant zombie blowfly swooped in again, almost knocking Zack over.

Zack poked it in the eye with the branch.

Hard.

So hard, in fact, that black jelly spurted out all over him. "Gross!" said Zack, jumping backward as the giant mutant zombie blowfly buzzed angrily and flew away.

Zack hated giant mutant zombie blowflies. Almost as much as he hated the Great White Butt.

"Zack!" whispered his butt.

"What is it?" said Zack, stopping to wipe large handfuls of the zombie blowfly's gooey eyeball slime off his clothes.

"Don't you think it's kind of strange that a butt would choose to live out here all by itself?"

Zack — whose sense of what was strange had in the past few months undergone a similar expansion to his sense of what was dangerous — shrugged. "But it didn't choose to live here," he said, warily watching for the zombie blowfly's return. "It was sucked into a brown hole!"

"So it says," said his butt. "But it could be lying. It could be leading us into some sort of trap. It could be working for the Great White Buttosaurs. We could be sacrifices!"

"Good theory," said Zack. "But you're forgetting one thing. We *asked* it to take us to the Crack of Doom. And it tried to talk us out of it."

"I don't like it," muttered Zack's butt. "I don't like it at all. . . ."

"Relax," said Zack. "It's harmless. And, you've got to admit, kind of cute."

"Cute!?" said Zack's butt, flushing red. "Are you kidding?"

"Are you blushing?" said Zack.

"As if," said Zack's butt, flushing even redder.

"You *are* blushing!" said Zack. "You know what I think?"

"No," said Zack's butt, "and I'm not interested."

But Zack was on a roll. "I think," he said, "I think you like . . ."

"ZACK!" yelled his butt. "Watch out!"

CHAPTER THIRTY-FIVE

Poopasaur

Zack froze before he could finish the sentence. Out of the corner of his eye he saw a dark shape lunging toward him. At first he thought it was the zombie blowfly returning, but then he noticed that it was the wrong color.

It was brown.

With big teeth.

And bad breath.

And an even worse temper.

CHOMP!

The brown monster's jaws snapped down hard just a few millimeters short of Zack's nose. The stench of its breath brought tears to Zack's eyes. Before he could do anything, however, the brown monster reared back and lunged forward for another bite.

Zack stared.

It was ugly. *Really* ugly. It had two tiny black eyes and

an enormous mouth. Its chunky brown skin was cracked like dried-out mud.

It struck again.

Zack threw himself face first onto the ground.

Again, the monster's teeth closed on air.

The others were too far ahead to be of any help.

"Well, don't just stand there!" Zack yelled at his terrified butt. "Do something!"

"What?" said Zack's butt.

"Anything!" said Zack.

Zack's butt began to dance. "You put your left hand in, you put your left hand out . . ." it sang.

"Anything *but* the hokey pokey!" yelled Zack, as he watched the enormous brown serpentlike creature rearing back for a third attack.

Zack's butt picked up a stick and, using it as a cane, began a rudimentary tap dance.

"Not *that*, either!" said Zack.

"But I don't know any other dances!" said Zack's butt.

The monster hurled itself forward.

Zack, reeling under the withering blast of its breath, rolled over onto his back and prepared to kick it.

But there was nothing to kick.

It was all mouth.

Just as the brown monster was about to engulf Zack, however, their guide butt appeared.

It bent over, took aim, and fired.

The monster's head snapped backward. With a yelp it

withdrew back into the jungle as quickly and mysteriously as it had emerged.

Zack sat up, blinking. "Thanks," he said.

"Are you all right?" said the butt.

"I think so," said Zack. "What *was* that?"

"A poopasaur," it said. "There are a lot of them around this year."

"A poopasaur?" said Zack.

"'Big, lumbering, and deadly,'" said Ned, reading from his book as he rushed toward them. "'Lives in cocobutt-tree forests. Prone to jumping out from undergrowth unexpectedly.'"

"Gee, lucky you brought that book, Ned," said Zack, shaking his head. "I never would have guessed otherwise."

"Just trying to be helpful," said Ned.

"Keep your eyes open, everybody," announced their guide. "This is a dangerous place."

As they resumed walking, Zack's butt tapped Zack on the leg.

"That was no accident, Zack," it said. "It's trying to kill us."

"How do you figure that?" said Zack. "That butt just saved me from a poopasaur. Which is more than I can say for you!"

Zack's butt reddened. "Yeah, well, how come it didn't say anything about poopasaurs before?"

"It tried to convince us that it was too dangerous to go to the Crack of Doom in the first place," said Zack.

"But it didn't warn us about poopasaurs!" said Zack's butt. "Not specifically."

"Well, no," said Zack. "But . . ."

"See what I mean?" said his butt. "This is not a butt to be trusted."

Zack shrugged. "We don't have much choice," he said.

CHAPTER THIRTY-SIX

Campfire

That night the three butt-fighters and two butts sat around a small campfire. Long, low poop-asaur mating calls filled the air.

Zack looked up into the blackness and marveled at the awesome wash of stars above them. It was all so beautiful, he thought. It was hard to believe that a life-on-Earth-destroying arseteroid could come out of such a sky. But it was definitely coming. And soon.

Ned and Eleanor were roasting cocobutts the size of baseballs. "These are much bigger than the cocobutts back home," said Ned, spitting out small pieces of the shell as he spoke.

"I know," said their guide. "Buttolution is not always for the better."

"You can say that again," said Zack's butt. "Butts would have been so much better off without heads messing things up."

Zack ignored his butt's remark and turned to their guide. "So, how did you come to be here, exactly?" said Zack. "I know you got sucked into a brown hole, but what were you doing out in space to begin with?"

"Well," said the butt, staring into the fire, "it's a sad story. I used to have an owner. A really good one. She took care of me. Clothed me. Wiped me. Even let me watch television occasionally. She was the best owner a butt could ever want. But then one day I woke up and she wasn't there. I wasn't in her bed. I was in a trash can. I'd been cut loose. Discarded. Abandoned."

"Zack would never do that to *me*," said Zack's butt. "Would you, Zack?"

Zack raised his eyebrows. "Wouldn't I?" he said.

Zack's butt ignored Zack. "You must have done something pretty bad," it said to the other butt.

"I never did anything!" said the butt. "At first I thought there must have been some mistake — some terrible misunderstanding. Had I not done everything I could do to be a good and faithful butt? Had I not fulfilled my half of the charter between a butt and its owner? I searched and searched for her but, alas, it was in vain. She had simply disappeared. Vanished."

"That's too bad," said Ned quietly.

Zack noticed that Eleanor was staring intently at the small butt through the smoke.

He supposed the butt's story couldn't have been easy for her to listen to. He knew how much she regretted her decision to cut her own butt loose all those years ago. Back then it had been a routine procedure for butt-fighters to replace their butts with false ones. No butt-fighter wanted to have their butt-fighting ability compromised by a butt that might not be completely loyal. But that was before she'd seen Zack and his butt in action — before she'd realized what a powerful team a butt and its owner could really be.

The small pink butt wiped a tear from its cheek.

"So, what did you do then?" Zack asked the butt gently.

"I kept looking," it said. "I wandered the solar system searching for her. I would have kept searching, too, but I got sucked into the brown hole and deposited here, with no way of getting back. But to tell you the truth, I'm not sure I'd *want* to go back, even if I could. I can be lonely here just as well as there. Besides, I'm not sure I'd recognize my owner now even if I did see her again. She was a little girl, then — she'd be quite grown up by now."

The butt fell silent.

The fire glowed low.

Something screeched in the distance.

It was the saddest story that Zack had ever heard.

Ned and Eleanor were both wiping their eyes.

Even Zack's butt was choked up. "Do you have a tissue, Zack?" it whispered.

"Sure," said Zack, pulling a tissue from his pocket and handing it to his butt.

"I hope you find your owner some day," said Zack.

The butt shrugged. "Thanks," it said. "You're nice. You don't need a spare, do you?"

Zack's butt bristled. "No, he's doing just fine for now, thanks," it said.

"You're lucky to have an owner like him," said the butt.

"True," said Zack's butt. "But he's even luckier to have a butt like me."

Zack glanced at Eleanor. She seemed even sadder than before.

"We'd better get some sleep," said the butt. "We have a lot of ground to cover tomorrow."

"Sleep?" said Zack's butt. "With tyrannosore-arses, tricerabutts, giant stinkants, and poopasaurs out there . . . I'm not going to sleep a wink."

"Good!" said their guide. "Then you're on guard duty. Keep the fire burning and whatever you do, *don't fall asleep*. Understand?"

"There's not much chance of that," said Zack's butt.

"What, not much chance of you understanding or not much chance of you falling asleep?" said their guide.

"Ha ha, very funny," said Zack's butt. "Goodnight."

Zack, Ned, and Eleanor hunkered down on their cocobutt-tree leaf beds and were asleep within minutes.

Five minutes later the guide butt dozed off.

And, five minutes after that, so did Zack's butt.

CHAPTER THIRTY-SEVEN

Stinkant-Napped

It was dark when Zack awoke.

He blinked a few times and tried to remember where he was. He had been so tired that he hardly even remembered falling asleep. One moment he'd been studying Eleanor's sad face across the smoke of the campfire and the next moment . . . well . . . now he was lying in pitch darkness.

He shut his eyes tightly and opened them again.

He'd had a dream, he remembered that much.

A crazy dream.

He'd dreamed that the fire had gone out and that a gigantic red stinkant had picked him up in its pincers and carried him off to an underground stinkant nest.

As Zack remembered his dream it seemed so vivid that he could actually hear the scuttling and digging noises the stinkants made.

And he could smell the dank earth of the underground nest.

Where was the fire? he wondered.

As they'd been setting up camp the previous evening their guide butt had made a big deal out of the importance of fire in protecting them from the night-time predators of the prehistoric world. But now the fire was completely out.

He looked up.

Before he'd gone to sleep there'd been a stunning canopy of stars above them.

Now there was nothing.

No fire.

No stars.

No sky.

What was going on?

Zack became aware of a pain around his waist. A dull, aching pain. The sort of pain that you might have felt if you'd been picked up by, say, a pair of giant stinkant pincers. . . .

Oh no, thought Zack. "Eleanor?" he said. "Are you awake?"

"Zack?" said Eleanor groggily. "What happened to the fire?"

"I'm afraid I've got some bad news," said Zack.

"What now?" said Eleanor.

"I think we've been stinkant-napped," said Zack. "We may be in great danger."

The scuttling sounds grew louder. Whatever was making them was definitely coming closer.

"Have you got a match?" said Zack.

"Yeah," said Eleanor. "Hang on."

Eleanor struck the match.

"Uh-oh," said Eleanor as the tiny yellow glow confirmed Zack's worst fears. "I think you're right."

Zack nodded as he looked around. They were in an underground chamber with rough-hewn rock walls. Just the two of them. His butt was missing.

So was Ned.

And so was their guide.

"How do we get out of here?" said Eleanor, striking another match.

"Same way we got in, I guess," said Zack.

"And how was that?" said Eleanor.

"I don't know," said Zack. "I was asleep. Sort of."

"Ouch," said Eleanor. The match she was holding had burned down to her fingertips. She pulled another from the pack, struck it, and peered into the darkness.

"What's that?" she said.

"What?" said Zack.

"On the wall over there — it looks like writing," said Eleanor. "I'm going to go and see what it says."

"I'm coming with you," said Zack, who was getting a little creeped out by the darkness and the scuttling sounds.

The two butt-fighters tripped and stumbled their way across the rocky floor to the far wall of the cave.

Zack's eyes stung.

At the rock face, Eleanor lit a match and leaned in close.

They were words all right.

Words smeared on the wall in a wet, glistening paste.

Zack began reading aloud: "'Warning! The Great White Butt is . . .'"

His voice faltered as he recognized the words.

"That's the warning Ned saw!" said Eleanor. "Only these words aren't millions of years old. They're *fresh*!"

The match in Eleanor's hand went out.

"They might be fresh," said Zack. "But we're still too late."

Suddenly Zack was blinded by a flashlight shone directly into his eyes.

"You're not too late yet, soldier!" said a voice. "But you certainly took your time."

Although Zack couldn't see a thing, he had no trouble identifying the voice.

"Gran!" he said. "Is that you?"

CHAPTER THIRTY-EIGHT

Gran

Of course it's me!" said Gran.

"And me!" said the Forker.

"And me!" said the Flicker.

"But didn't you . . . don't you all . . . *die* here?" said Zack, struggling with the complications of time travel.

"First I've heard about it," said Gran. "Unless you know something that I don't."

Zack gulped . . . and quickly shook his head.

"Pincher," said Eleanor, quickly changing the subject, "it's great to see you, but can you shine that flashlight someplace else — it hurts!"

"Sorry," said Gran, lowering her flashlight.

"Where are we?" said Zack.

"We're in a stinkant nest," said Gran. "Where do you think? Ferocious darn critters. A lot bigger than the ones back in my day. I mean, the ones *to come* in my day . . . when I'm born, that is. Darn this time travel! It does my head in!"

"Look, it's *simple*," said the Forker. "We've been over it and over it and over it! You were born in the future. Then you came back here to the past. But just because you are in the past doesn't mean that you *weren't* born in the future — it just means that you haven't been born in the future *yet* — not technically anyway — even though you *were* because how could you be here if you *weren't*? Understand?"

"No, I don't," said Gran. "How could I be born in the future?"

"You *weren't* born in the future!" said the Forker. "For goodness sakes!"

"Language!" said Gran.

"'Goodness' is not a swear word!" said the Forker.

"No, but I don't like the tone of your voice," said Gran. "I'll thank you to remember your manners."

"Sorry," said the Forker. "All I was trying to say was that you weren't born in the future."

"But you told me I was," said Gran.

"What he means," said the Flicker helpfully, "is that you *were* born in the future, but when you were born the future wasn't the future. It was the present. Not the *present* present, of course. The *future* present. But nevertheless, the present in which no past or future exists. Where the confusion comes in is that from where we stand at the moment, *that* present is our future. Get it?"

"So I was born in . . . the present?" said Gran.

"Yes, the *future* present," said the Flicker triumphantly. "Which is now in *our* past, of course."

"So I was born in our past future present," said Gran. "Now I'm even more confused than ever!"

"It doesn't matter!" said Eleanor, impatiently.

"It may not matter to you, young lady," said Gran, "but my birth matters a great deal to me!"

"I'm sorry," said Eleanor. "Your birth matters a great deal to me, too, it's just that we're running out of time. When did you last see the Great White Butt?"

"We were spat out of the brown hole right behind him," said Gran, "straight into the middle of a crowd of giant mutant zombie blowflies. Luckily they concealed our arrival and we were able to hide. We heard him talking to himself — ranting and raving about how he was going to get revenge and send the Great White Buttosaurs back through the brown hole to Buttageddonize the future Earth. We tracked him as far as we could but then we got chased by an enormous hairy butt."

"It was horrible," said the Flicker. "Took every towel I had to keep it at bay."

"And every fork on my belt!" said the Forker.

"Yes," nodded Gran. "It gave us a run for our money. But by the time we'd given it the shake we'd lost the Great White Butt's trail."

"We were trying to find the Great White Butt again when we were surrounded by stinkants," said the Forker. "They brought us here. We tried to escape, but there were just too many of them. Then we had the idea of killing a stinkant and using its blood as paint to send you a warning about Buttageddon."

"But how did you know we would see your message?" said Zack. "It was deep underground in the

Great Windy Desert. Ned Smelly only found it by sheer accident."

"*Accident* is just another word for *fate*, Zack," said Gran, suddenly reminding Zack of a witch in the dim gloom of the cave. "Don't you remember what the Blind Butt-feeler foretold? She said that you will free not just the world, but the entire univarse from the scourge of butts past, present, AND future!"

The words struck Zack like a triple lightning bolt: "I know that's what she said," said Zack slowly. "But what does 'past, present, and future' mean, exactly?"

"Oh that's easy," said the Flicker. "Let me explain. . . ."

"No!" said Eleanor. "Not now. Something's coming. Play dead! And switch off the flashlight!"

CHAPTER THIRTY-NINE

Reunited

The butt-fighters dropped to the ground.

They could hear scuffling and shouting coming from the passage outside.

"Put me down!" yelled a shrill voice. "Put me down!"

Zack smiled. "That's my butt!" he said.

"Shhh!" hissed Eleanor.

"Wait until my owner finds out about this!" Zack's butt said. "He'll tear this nest apart looking for me. And when he finds me he'll rip you to pieces!"

Zack heard a loud thud.

And then another.

"Ouch!" said his butt.

"Oof!" said a voice that Zack recognized as Ned's.

The butt-fighters listened as the scuttling receded back up the passage.

"You can run, but you can't hide!" yelled Zack's butt

fiercely. "You'll be sorry you ever messed with Zack Freeman's butt!"

"Steady there," said Ned. "I hate to be a party pooper, but a typical stinkant colony can consist of up to two hundred thousand stinkants and can have anywhere between ten thousand and twenty thousand food and egg chambers. Even if we *could* locate Zack and Eleanor — which is highly unlikely — it wouldn't be enough. It would take a small army of butt-fighters to fight our way out of here."

"Which is exactly what we have, soldier!" said Gran, flicking on her flashlight.

"Mrs. Freeman?" said Ned, picking himself up off the cave floor and throwing his arms around her. "Am I glad to see you!"

"How are you, Ned?" she said. "I haven't seen you since you were a boy. And now look at you!"

"Yeah," said Ned. "Come a long way, haven't I? Stuck in a stinkant nest in sixty-five million years BC."

"Your mother would be proud," said Gran. "Meet the Flicker and the Forker!"

The butt-fighters shook hands.

"Pleased to meet you," said the Flicker.

"We've heard a lot about you," said the Forker.

"And I've heard a great deal about you!" said Ned. He noticed Eleanor and Zack. "There you are! Good to see you both!"

"Zack!" said Zack's butt, jumping into Zack's arms.

"Where's our guide?" asked Eleanor.

"We don't know," said Ned. "Not with us. I take it it's not with you?"

"No," said Eleanor. "I hope it's all right."

"Hmmph," said Zack's butt. "I'm *sure* it is."

"What makes you say that?" said Eleanor, studying Zack's butt quizzically.

"Don't you get it?" said Zack's butt. "It double-crossed us."

"Double-crossed us?" said Eleanor. "What do you mean?"

"It was obviously working for the stinkants all along. If I ever see that thing again I'll kill it!"

"That's highly unlikely," said Ned. "This place is like a maze. Took me a week to map the whole nest comprehensively. Even if you *did* know where it was, you'd be stinkant-meat long before you'd be able to locate it and kill it."

"You've been here before?" said the Flicker.

"Yes," said Ned. "This is where I found your warning."

"Do you still have the map?" said the Flicker hopefully.

"No," said Ned. "Not on me. It's in . . ."

"Shh!" said Eleanor. "Listen!"

The scuttling in the passage outside the holding cave was getting louder.

And somewhere, far above them, they could hear the sound of muffled explosions.

CHAPTER FORTY

Stomp!

Robobutt!" said Ned, his eyes shining.

"We don't know that for sure," said Eleanor.

"It's got to be!" said Ned.

"But even if it is Robobutt, how will she find us?" said Zack. "You said yourself there are at least ten thousand separate chambers."

"Heat sensors," said Ned.

"Yes, but how did she know we were in the stinkant nest in the first place?" said Zack's butt.

"That I *don't* know," said Ned, frowning.

The explosions were getting louder. Smoke and acrid fumes filled the air.

"Don't worry," said Gran. "We'll take care of it."

"Yeah!" said the Flicker, cracking a rolled-up dish towel in front of him. "This 'Robobutt' will regret the day it ever messed with me."

"You mean *us*," said the Forker, brandishing a large barbecue fork in his hand like a Japanese ninja sword.

"No," said Ned. "You don't understand! Robobutt is our friend, not an enemy. I built her. She's a state-of-the-art butt-fighting machine in the shape of a Great White Butt!"

"Well, good for you, Ned!" said Gran. "You always were a bit of a tinkerer."

"A butt-fighting robot!" said the Flicker, letting his towel fall to his side. "Now that I'd like to see!"

"Sounds like we soon will," said the Forker, re-holstering his fork.

The scuttling sound of the stinkants was getting louder. Zack could feel the earth trembling all around them. Robobutt was not so much navigating the passages of the nest as completely destroying them.

As the glare of daylight lit up the passage outside their cave, a river of stinkants surged past the opening. A lethal river of shiny red and black abdomens, thoraxes, legs, and razor-sharp jaws. All rushing to attack Robobutt.

The smell was horrible, and not helped by the fact that Robobutt was incinerating her attackers as she made her way toward the cave holding the butt-fighters.

Huge hissing blasts of flaming insect repellent and thick acrid smoke filled the air. As Robobutt came closer, the river of stinkants began to back up and then flow into the cave chamber.

"Everybody against the wall!" commanded Gran, as Robobutt made a dramatic entrance.

The front line of stinkants reared back, snapping their jaws and squirting jets of foul-smelling juice at Robobutt.

"Stand clear, please," said Robobutt in a calm and authoritative tone. "Stand clear."

But the stinkants did not stand clear. If anything, they redoubled their efforts.

"You were warned," explained Robobutt matter-of-factly. "Have it your way!"

CHAPTER FORTY-ONE

Escape?

Zack hoped Robobutt wasn't about to blast the stinkants with a burst of flaming insect repellent. She was too close.

Everyone in the chamber would be incinerated.

But Robobutt had obviously already taken that into consideration.

Instead of using fire, she simply started stomping.

The stinkants in the front line didn't stand a chance.

Robobutt's powerful feet smashed through their tough armor, sending their putrid payloads of hot, sticky stinkant juice splattering all over the chamber.

The stinkants pushed back further.

The butt-fighters were backed up against the wall — the Forker jabbing the ants with his fork and the Flicker flicking them with his rolled-up dish towel to prevent the frenzied mass from crushing them against the rock.

But Robobutt kept stomping relentlessly until all of the stinkants in the chamber had been destroyed and all the stinkants outside the chamber were too scared — or too smart — to come in.

"Good work, Robobutt!" said Ned. "You're a hero!"

"Just doing the job I was programmed to do," said Robobutt.

"But how did you defeat those tyrannosore-arses?" said Eleanor. "They looked like they were going to rip apart your fully riveted reinforced steel cheeks."

"They did not know who they were dealing with," said Robobutt. "I am Robobutt. Fully riveted reinforced steel cheeks. Turbo-assisted jet repulsion units. Nuclear wart-head equipped. Matter transport assisted entry and exit. Inside and outside voice options. Onboard tea- and coffee-making facilities. And I am self-wiping!!"

Eleanor nodded. "Of course," she said. "Silly me. How could I have forgotten?"

"But how did you know we were in the stinkant nest?" said Ned.

"I was alerted to this fact by a cute pink butt," said Robobutt. "It claims it was acting as your guide."

"I knew it wouldn't abandon us!" said Eleanor, flashing an *I told you so* glance at Zack's butt. "Where is it now?"

"It is inside my control center," said Robobutt. "I couldn't have found you without it. But enough talk. I advise immediate departure. Repeat. *Immediate* departure.

Reinforcements are already on their way. Prepare for teleportation."

As Robobutt said this, she beamed her teleporting light down to where the butt-fighters were standing.

"Come on, Gran," said Zack. "Step into the light."

"No, Zack," said Gran, shaking her head sadly.

CHAPTER FORTY-TWO

Good-bye

But you're coming with us," said Zack as he studied his Gran's tired face. "Aren't you?"

"No," said Gran. "At least, not yet. You see, we haven't finished our message to you. We'd run out of stinkant-blood paint, but with all these stinkant carcasses we've got all we need to finish the job."

"But it doesn't matter about the message anymore!" said Zack. "We already got it!"

"That's true," said the Forker. "But only because we're staying behind to finish it. If we don't finish it now, you won't be *able* to get it in the future, thus condemning the Earth to certain Buttageddon."

"But the nest has been destroyed!" said Zack.

"Not all of it," said Ned. "And there are still plenty of stinkants left to rebuild it."

"But . . ." said Zack.

"Don't worry about us," said the Flicker. "We can look after ourselves. We'll catch up with you later."

"No, you won't," said Zack. "If you stay you'll die here — all of you — we know because . . . because . . . *Ned saw your bones.*"

Gran put her hand on Zack's shoulder. "We all have to die sometime," she said.

"Yes, I know," said Zack. "But not *now*! First you, then my parents and now you . . . *again*! I'll be all alone."

"Your parents?" said Gran, her fingers tightening on Zack's shoulder. "James and Judi are dead? How?"

"They were squashed by a giant brown blob," said Zack sadly. "At the start of Buttageddon. *Everybody* was squashed — only a few of us made it out."

Gran looked older and frailer as she absorbed the news. Then a change passed over her face — a look of cold determination. "Then it's all the more important that we stay here and finish our task," she said, hugging Zack. "Goodbye, Zack. And good luck. The future of the world — and your parents — depends on you."

"Gee, no pressure or anything," said Zack's butt.

"Advise immediate departure," said Robobutt. "I can sense reinforcements on the way. Prepare for immediate teleportation and departure."

"Come on, Zack!" said Eleanor, leading him into the light. "We have to go."

Zack slowly let his gran go and stood in the teleportation beam with the others. Then, just before he dematerialized, he rushed back to Gran. He reached into his pocket and pulled out the cake of soap Ned had found in the cave. "Here!" he said. "This belongs to you."

"Thanks, Zack," said Gran. "You're a good boy."

Zack nodded and resumed his place under the light, tears in his eyes.

CHAPTER FORTY-THREE

Questions

As they rematerialized in the safety of Robobutt's control room, they were greeted by their guide butt.

"You!" said Zack's butt.

"I'm very glad you're all right!" said Eleanor, rushing to its side.

"I'm very happy to see you all again," it replied. "I thought I might have been too late."

Zack's butt eyed it suspiciously. "How come you weren't stinkant-napped like the rest of us?" it said.

"I'm a very light sleeper," said the butt. "But even so, the stinkants were fast. By the time I realized what was happening it was all I could do to save myself."

"Gosh, imagine that," said Zack's butt.

The butt shot Zack's butt an angry look. "The real question," it said, "is how come *you* fell asleep and let the fire go out? You were on guard. It was your responsibility!"

"I just shut my eye for a second," said Zack's butt, shuffling its feet. "I was tired."

"We all were," said the butt. "It's no excuse. You shouldn't have volunteered for guard duty if you weren't capable of staying awake."

"I *didn't* volunteer for guard duty," said Zack's butt. "You *forced* me to do it."

"I didn't force you to do anything!" said the butt. "You could have said no."

"I was too tired," said Zack's butt. "I didn't know what I was saying."

"Never mind," said Ned. "What's done is done, and arguing about what *was* done won't undo it." He turned to the guide. "What I want to know is, how did you know about Robobutt?"

"I *didn't*," said the butt. "Robobutt found me. She was already looking for you. I just guided her here. All I really knew was that it would be the only way you could possibly be rescued from a stinkant nest."

"I'm so proud of you!" said Eleanor. "Well done!"

"Yes," said Ned. "Thank you."

"Don't thank me," said the butt. "Thank Robobutt." Zack's butt muttered something inaudible.

"I beg your pardon?" said the butt.

"Excuse me," said Zack's butt, turning away and walking over to Zack.

Zack was standing in front of the screen watching his gran and the Forker and the Flicker resume their work on the wall as Robobutt reversed out of the cave.

Eleanor came and stood beside him.

"We'll never see them again, will we?" said Zack.

"If I've learned anything in the last twenty-four hours," said Eleanor, "it's never to say never."

"But why did they *all* have to stay?" said Zack.

"Because that's the way it happened," said Eleanor. "We can't change that. Besides, if your gran's soap wasn't there, we would have thought Ned Smelly was just suffering methane madness. It all fits."

"But we're trying to change the Great White Butt's evacuation plan," said Zack.

"Some things we can change, others we can't," said Eleanor. "It's just the way it is."

"Maybe we won't be able to change the evacuation plan, either," said Zack.

"No," said Eleanor. "And then again, maybe we will."

CHAPTER FORTY-FOUR

Confrontation

Robobutt wasted no time extracting herself and her passengers from the stinkant nest.

Although the fighting was intense and at least another thirty thousand unfortunate stinkants were stomped on or incinerated, Robobutt eventually broke free, roaring up into the primeval dawn.

"Next stop, Crack of Doom," she announced.

"No," said Zack's butt. "Next stop right now! We have a passenger to drop off."

"What are you talking about?" said Zack. "You can't get off!"

"Not *me*," said his butt, pointing at their guide. "Her!"

"Me?" said their guide. "What did I do?"

"It's what you *didn't* do that's the problem," said Zack's butt. "You didn't protect us from the stinkants!"

"I tried to!" said the guide. "I put *you* on watch. It was *you* who fell asleep. If it's anyone's fault it's *yours*."

"It was all part of your evil plan!" said Zack's butt.

"What evil plan?" said Eleanor.

"Isn't it obvious?" said Zack's butt. "It's working for the stinkants. It knew I wouldn't be able to stay awake. And while I slept it told them where to find us."

"That's ridiculous," said the guide. "I came to save you, remember?"

Zack's butt hesitated for a moment, but it was on a roll and nothing could stop it.

"That was part of your evil plan, too," said Zack's butt. "You instructed the stinkants to capture us so you could save us so we wouldn't suspect that you put them up to it."

"Listen to yourself!" said the guide. "You're talking nonsense. Why would I be working for the stinkants? And even if I was, why would I care whether you knew it was me once you were captured?"

"I don't know!" said Zack's butt. "But that's exactly what I intend to find out!"

"You're crazy," said the guide.

"And you're a dirty double-crossing stinkant-butt-kissing loser with no friends!"

The guide's cheeks flushed red with anger. "You take that back!" it said.

"Make me!" said Zack's butt.

"With pleasure!" said the guide, launching itself at Zack's butt.

The two butts began scrapping on the floor — like wild dogs — in front of the stunned butt-fighters. It happened so fast that nobody had time to stop them.

Even Robobutt was caught off guard. "Butt-fight on deck!" she announced, a little belatedly, as Zack's butt grabbed the guide in a double-handed cheek-lock and started to stretch it until it looked like it would tear in two.

"I'll kill you!" said Zack's butt.

"Stop it!" yelled Eleanor, throwing a bucket of cold water onto the fighting butts.

The shock made Zack's butt lose its grip, and the two butts fell apart, panting heavily.

Zack immediately stepped down and grabbed his butt's arm and twisted it up behind its back.

"Ow! Ow! Ow!" it yelled. "Stop!"

"Only if you promise to stop fighting," said Zack.

"Okay," said his butt. "I'll stop . . ." Zack released his butt's arm. It immediately leaped at the guide and started fighting again. "I'll stop when it's dead!"

"Zack! Control your butt!" said Eleanor, picking up the small pink butt and holding it above her head while Zack's butt jumped up and down underneath it, snapping angrily. "Leave it alone, you maniac!" she said, booting Zack's butt in the left cheek.

"You stay out of this," said Zack's butt. "This is between us — it's got nothing to do with you!"

"That's where you're wrong," said Eleanor. "It's got everything to do with me."

"Oh yeah?" said Zack's butt. "And why is that?"

"Because," said Eleanor.

"Because why?" said Zack's butt.

"Because," said Eleanor, "it's *my butt*."

CHAPTER FORTY-FIVE

Truth

Eleanor's words stopped the fight more effectively than any number of buckets of cold water could have.

"*Your* butt?" said Zack's butt.

"*Your* butt?" said Zack.

"*Your* butt?" said Ned.

"*Your* butt?" said Robobutt.

"*Your* butt?" said Eleanor's butt.

"Yes," said Eleanor. "*My* butt."

CHAPTER FORTY-SIX

Abandoned

But . . . but . . . why didn't you say anything?" said Eleanor's butt. "Didn't you recognize me?"

"I recognized you right away," said Eleanor. "I wanted to say something, but I didn't know how to. Or how you'd feel about me. I thought you might be angry."

"Angry?" said her butt, reddening. "Who, me? *Angry?* Why should I be *angry?* I only tried to serve you as well as I knew how. I only tried to be there for you when you needed me. I only tried to be a good, solid, reliable, honest butt and what did I get for my trouble? What did I get for my pain? What did I get for doing all the work that no other part of your body would — or could — do? I'll tell you what I got — chucked into a trash can without so much as a thank-you note! So why should I be angry? Of course I'm not angry. In fact, I don't think I can remember when I've ever felt quite so *not-angry!*"

"I'm sorry," said Eleanor. "But I didn't realize what I was doing. When the Great White Butt killed my mother, I knew I had to become a butt-fighter and that would mean having to get a false butt. . . . I didn't know then what I know now: that butt-fighters and their butts can work together. That a butt can be a butt-fighter's best friend."

"So that's all you want me back for," said her butt. "To make you a better butt-fighter. You just don't get it, do you?"

"No, that's not what I meant!" said Eleanor. "I can understand how you feel, but . . ."

"No, you can't," said her butt. "You have no idea how it feels to be abandoned. But don't worry, you soon will."

"What do you mean?" said Eleanor.

"Robobutt!" said Eleanor's butt. "Stop immediately! I'm getting off."

"Affirmative," said Robobutt. "Landing now!"

"But you can't get off," said Eleanor.

"And why not?" said Eleanor's butt.

"Because we'll never find the Crack of Doom without you!" said Eleanor.

"And?" said her butt.

"And what?" said Eleanor.

"And?" repeated her butt.

"And because you're my butt," said Eleanor. "I need you."

"Right answer," said her butt, "just a little bit too late. Goodbye, Eleanor. I'm sorry it didn't work out between us."

"Robobutt has landed," said Robobutt. "Safe to depart."

"Teleport me out, please, Robobutt," said Eleanor's butt.

Eleanor watched sadly as her butt disappeared under the light.

"Good riddance, I say," muttered Zack's butt quietly. But not quietly enough.

"Shut up!" snarled Eleanor. "Or . . . or . . ."

"Or what?" said Zack's butt.

"Or *else*," said Eleanor.

"Did you hear that, Zack?" said his butt. "She threatened me."

"*Shut up!*" said Zack.

CHAPTER FORTY-SEVEN

Stuck!

Eleanor glared fiercely at Zack's butt. "You're nothing but a troublemaker," she said. "How are we supposed to find the Crack of Doom now?"

"Hey, don't blame me," said Zack's butt. "It's your butt that's the troublemaker."

"How dare you!" said Eleanor. "*You're* the one who fell asleep on your watch. And if my memory serves me correctly, wasn't it *you* who ran away in the first place to help the Great White Butt build his buttcano? And you have the nerve to call *my* butt a troublemaker?"

"Easy, Eleanor," said Zack. "That's all in the past now."

"And in case you hadn't noticed, chucklehead," said Eleanor, "so are we! We're stuck here without a map and now, thanks to your butt, no guide, either!"

"Negative," said Robobutt. "That is not correct. I can act as your guide."

"But you've never been here before," said Eleanor.

"You might have a BPS* system, but there are no satel-lites here — they haven't been invented yet. So as far as I can figure you're as lost as the rest of us."

"Negative," said Robobutt. "Although my BPS is cur-rently not functioning, I am equipped with many other features. Let me remind you that I am a Robobutt. Fully riveted reinforced steel cheeks. Turbo-assisted jet repul-sion units. Nuclear wart-head equipped . . ."

"Spare us the details," interrupted Eleanor.

"As you please," said Robobutt, undaunted by Eleanor's abruptness. "My sensors indicate an abnormal concen-tration of methane in the mountainous region to our northeast. I believe this is where the Crack of Doom will be found."

"How can you be sure?" said Ned. "With all these pre-historic butts running around, wouldn't there be an abnormal concentration of methane over the entire planet?"

"The molecular signature of this particular methane is almost identical to that emitted by the Great White Butt," said Robobutt. "I believe there is a ninety-five per-cent probability of it belonging to a large number of the same types of Great White Butt. Furthermore, it almost exactly corresponds with coordinates of where the arse-teroid that wiped out life on Earth hit. Given that all but one of the Great White Buttosaurs was destroyed in that impact it strongly suggests this is the spot."

"All right then," said Zack. "What are we waiting for?"

Eleanor shrugged.

*Butt positioning system. See glossary.

Ned nodded. "Proceed to the Crack of Doom, Robobutt," he said.

"Affirmative!" said Robobutt, roaring into action. "Prepare for liftoff."

Zack grabbed a handrail as Robobutt rose into the air. But as fast as she had risen, Robobutt returned to the ground.

"What's the matter, Robobutt?" said Ned.

"Sorry," said Robobutt. "I seem to be experiencing some difficulty. Prepare for relaunch."

Robobutt rose into the air again, higher this time, but only for a few seconds before crashing to the ground once more.

"Liftoff status report!" said Ned.

"My undercarriage appears to be stuck," said Robobutt.

"Full thrust!" said Ned. "Give it everything you've got."

"Affirmative!" said Robobutt, drawing on every bit of her nuclear stinkant-juice powered twin-injected nitro-assisted engine's power.

Zack and Eleanor both put their fingers in their ears to block out the deafening roar.

But still Robobutt remained Earthbound.

"Negative," said Robobutt. "Robobutt is immobilized. Recommend extra-vehicular excursion to establish and remove cause."

"I'll go," volunteered Zack.

"Way to go, Zack," said his butt, jumping up and slapping him on the back. "I knew we could count on you."

"You're coming with me, you know," said Zack. "I'm not going out there without backup. It's dangerous."

"That's exactly why I'd prefer to remain here," said his butt. "Why don't you take Eleanor? She'll be more use to you."

"Don't push your luck," said Eleanor with quiet menace.

Zack's butt saw the look in her eyes. "When do we leave?" it said.

"Right now," said Zack.

CHAPTER FORTY-EIGHT

Vines

Wow!" said Zack as he and his butt materialized onto the ground in front of Robobutt. "Would you look at that!"

Robobutt was perched on the edge of a deep canyon.

"That's some crack," said his butt admiringly.

"It's so deep!" said Zack, trying to see the bottom.

"It's so wide!" said his butt.

Zack stared down into it for so long that he began to feel light-headed. He had to force himself to stop looking and concentrate on the job at hand.

It wasn't too hard to see why Robobutt was unable to lift off.

She was caught in a messy tangle of pale gray vines. The vines were attached to a clump of trees and rocks and stretched right across the canyon like a giant spider web, except that the strands were as thick as rope.

"This stuff is everywhere," said Zack's butt. "What do you think it is?"

"Looks like some sort of vine or creeper," said Zack, taking a piece in his hand. "Pretty strong. And sticky, too. No wonder Robobutt couldn't break free."

Zack took his Butt-fighters' Army pocket knife out of his utility belt and began cutting.

It was hard work.

The vines were tough. They were made up of millions of strands wound tightly around each other to form a powerful bond.

As Zack cut slowly through the first vine — practically strand by strand — he was grateful for the stinkant juice, which had left a greasy coating on his hands. It allowed him to handle the vines without getting stuck to them.

He was halfway through cutting a second vine when he heard a voice.

It was a long way away, but definitely a voice.

"Can you hear that?" said Zack.

"Yes," said his butt. "And I can see where it's coming from too."

It pointed to the middle of the canyon.

Zack squinted.

There was something moving on the vines.

"Do you think it's Eleanor's butt?" said Zack.

"No," said Zack's butt. "It's not the right color. And it's too big."

"Do you think it's in trouble?" said Zack.

"It sounds like it," said Zack's butt.

"Do you think we should help it?" said Zack.

"Definitely not," said Zack's butt. "It's totally off-mission. I think we should just cut Robobutt free and get out of here."

"But," said Zack, "we can just leave it there!"

"Yes, we can," said Zack's butt, hacking into the vine. "This is a dangerous place. If we get distracted, we die."

They heard the strange gurgling cry again.

Zack looked at his butt. "What if it was you out there?" he said.

"But it's not me," said his butt.

"I know that," said Zack. "But *what if it was*? You'd want to be rescued, wouldn't you?"

"Y-yes . . ." said his butt. "But . . ."

"Then that settles it," said Zack. "We're going."

CHAPTER FORTY-NINE

Buttantula

Five minutes later Zack was crawling across the sticky vines toward the struggling figure, his butt perched on his shoulder.

"Gee," said his butt, looking down into the canyon. "I'd hate to fall."

"That makes two of us," said Zack.

"It's *such* a long way down," said his butt.

"Yep," said Zack, gripping the vine tightly.

"You'd end up totally splattered," said his butt. "Splattered just like a rotten watermelon dropped from a . . ."

"Would you shut up!" said Zack, grimacing. "You're not helping!"

Zack was all too well aware of how high they were.

And how far down they could fall.

But he was doing his best not to think about it. He

was just climbing slowly — and very carefully — across the vines toward the moaning figure.

"What's it saying?" said Zack's butt, as they crawled closer.

"I don't know," said Zack. "I don't know what language it's speaking. I don't even know what it is."

It didn't seem to resemble anything he'd ever seen before — man, beast, or butt — but, whatever it was, it was definitely trying to communicate with them.

It appeared to be made of flesh. Flesh that had been pulverized and mashed and then molded into the rough shape of a man.

And it stank.

Bad.

Really bad.

Although he was no stranger to bad smells, Zack gagged as they drew close to the horrible creature. It appeared to be trying to form words, but was having great trouble doing so because its mouth was so crudely formed — like a hole in a piece of dough.

"Can you make out what it's saying now?" said Zack's butt.

"Something about great danger, I think," said Zack.

"Um, Zack . . ." said his butt, the blood rushing from its cheeks, leaving it white and trembling and — for once — speechless.

"What's the matter?" said Zack. "Are you all right?"

His butt just pointed to the far side of the canyon.

An enormous black shape was moving across the vines toward them.

An enormous black shape with two bulbous domes and eight legs.

Zack didn't have Ned's *What Buttosaur Is That?* guide, but he didn't need it. He could see that it was a buttantula.

A *giant prehistoric* buttantula.

And suddenly — all too late — he could understand what the creature meant by "great danger."

One thing was for sure. There was no time to save the creature. It was every man — or in its case, every *mutant* — for himself.

Zack turned around, but the hideous creature grabbed his leg. "Don't leave me here," it begged. "Help me, Zack. Help me like I helped you!"

Zack froze.

The mutant knew his name!

CHAPTER FIFTY

Mutant

Zack stared at the mutant.

He looked into its eyes — two deep bloodshot pools of pain — and recognized their owner.

It was the Mutant Maggot Lord. Or, to be more accurate, thought Zack, what *used* to be the Mutant Maggot Lord. The mass of putrefying flesh in front of him bore little resemblance to anyone — or anything — but Zack knew those eyes.

He'd known them when they'd belonged to the Kisser — the dirty double-crossing traitor to the butt-fighting cause. And, even after the Kisser had become the hideously deformed Mutant Maggot Lord — as a result of falling into a brown lake full of giant mutant maggots — Zack had still recognized his eyes. And Zack had looked into those eyes, for what he'd been sure was the final time, when the Mutant Maggot Lord had heroically sacrificed himself to his beloved maggots in order to allow Zack, his butt, Eleanor, and the famous butt-fighting team of Mabel's Angels to escape to freedom. But what was he doing here? How was it possible that he was still alive? What had happened to this man . . . this beast . . . this . . . *mutant?*

"Zack!" yelled his butt, recovering its voice. "Do something!"

Zack looked up.

The buttantula was closing in fast.

Its twin cheeks wobbled sickeningly as it picked its way across its web. And its shiny black fangs glistened.

Zack reached out to the Mutant Maggot Lord and grabbed the arm that he was holding out to him. Zack pulled as hard as he could.

"Aaaggghhh!" yelled the Mutant Maggot Lord.

Zack gasped.

He'd ripped the Mutant Maggot Lord's arm completely off his body.

"Careful!" yelled the Mutant Maggot Lord. "I'm still very frail, you know."

"What on earth happened to you?" said Zack, staring disbelievingly at the dripping arm and then at the Mutant Maggot Lord.

"Now is hardly the time," said the Mutant Maggot Lord, "but as you know, I was eaten by mutant zombie maggots who then became mutant zombie blowflies. They got sucked into the brown hole. What you don't know is that they vomited me back up when they got here. I managed to pull the pieces of myself together again — or what was left of them — and then I got stuck in this stupid web."

"That's awful," said Zack, finding it impossible not to feel compassion for the former traitor. Not even a traitor deserved to be turned into a pile of zombie-blowfly barf.

"Yeah," said Zack's butt. "Awful and *totally gross.*"

A look of pain passed over what remained of the Mutant Maggot Lord's face.

"Sorry," said Zack. "My butt can be very rude. It doesn't mean it."

"Yes, I do!" said his butt.

"Don't worry about it," said the Mutant Maggot Lord, pointing. "Worry about that!"

Zack turned around.

The buttantula was close.

Too close.

CHAPTER FIFTY-ONE

Origami

The buttantula extended an enormous black leg toward Zack's heart. The lethal black tip shone like a spear.

Zack hit it with the only weapon he had available — the Mutant Maggot Lord's freshly amputated arm.

But it had no effect. He might as well have hit the buttantula with a stocking full of warm jelly. The arm splattered against the spider's leg and splashed all over Zack, his butt, and the Mutant Maggot Lord.

"Hey!" said the Mutant Maggot Lord. "That's my arm."

"That *was* your arm," said Zack's butt, wiping it off itself.

"Sorry," said Zack.

"Good one, Zack!" said his butt.

"Okay, Mr. Smarty Pants," said Zack. "I'd like to see you do better."

The tip of the spider's leg was only inches away from Zack's chest.

"All right, I will!" said Zack's butt. "Watch this!"

Zack gasped as he watched his butt leap from his shoulder onto the buttantula's leg and use it as a bridge to get right up close to its glistening black fangs. "Merry Christmas!" said Zack's butt, bending over and giving the buttantula a present it would never forget.

It had an instant effect. The huge beast withdrew its legs and contracted into a tight black ball as it tried to protect itself against the disgusting fumes.

"Phew," said Zack, blocking his nose. "What *have* you been eating?"

"You tell me!" said Zack's butt, leaping back onto his shoulder. "I'm just the delivery boy. Let's get out of here!"

"Good idea," said Zack, seizing the Mutant Maggot Lord's other arm — more gently this time. He pulled him free of the web and began climbing as quickly as he could back toward Robobutt.

He could see, with a mixture of surprise and relief, that Eleanor and Ned were outside the ship finishing the job of cutting Robobutt's legs free of the web.

"Hurry, Zack!" said his butt. "It's woken up!"

Zack, heart pounding, glanced behind him.

The buttantula, apparently recovered from its gassing and far more agile on the web, was bearing down on them. Fast.

It wasn't helping that Zack was burdened with the

combined weight of his butt and the Mutant Maggot Lord.

Zack looked up and saw the buttantula's fangs, like twin black tusks of death, bared and dripping with venom.

And then Zack did a strange thing.

He stopped, took what remained of his butt-fighter's certificate out of his utility belt, and began folding it.

"Are you out of your tiny butt-fighting mind, Zack?" yelled his butt. "Now is definitely not the time for origami."

"It's not origami," said Zack, smoothing it out and holding it up for his butt to see. "It's a paper plane. See?"

"Great, Zack," said his butt, in disbelief. "Well, it was nice knowing you. Right up to the point where you got methane madness."

"I don't have methane madness," said Zack. "Watch!"

Zack launched the paper plane. It flew, straight and true, right into one of the buttantula's eight brown eyes.

Once more it contracted in pain, giving Zack the crucial break he needed to reach the edge of the canyon, disentangle himself from the web, and run toward Robobutt.

Eleanor and Ned were just finishing cutting through the remaining strands of the web as Zack rushed up.

"Hey, that was my job," said Zack, panting.

"You're telling me!" said Eleanor. "What were you

thinking? You had one simple task and you decide to go buttantula hunting instead! What's the matter with you? And what's that?" Eleanor was pointing with one hand at the pile of putrid flesh cradled in Zack's arms, and blocking her nose with the other.

"An old friend," said Zack.

CHAPTER FIFTY-TWO

Trapped!

"Clear" said Ned, cutting through the last strand of web. "Everybody back inside."

As they assembled underneath Robobutt the buttantula was just reaching the edge of the canyon.

On the web it had moved fast, but on the ground it moved even faster.

"Teleport us up, Robobutt!" said Ned, staring at the rapidly advancing buttantula. "On the double!"

Zack felt Eleanor's hand clutch his arm tightly as the buttantula leaped at the huddled butt-fighters.

They dematerialized just in time.

Back inside Robobutt, Ned wasted no time. "Lift-off!" he commanded.

Robobutt, anticipating Ned's command, was already rising into the air.

"You can let go," said Zack to Eleanor, who was still holding his arm. "We're safe now."

"Oh, yes, of course," said Eleanor, quickly releasing her grip. "Sorry . . ." she said.

"It's okay," said Zack.

"No, it's *not* okay," said Eleanor, getting to her feet. "None of this is *okay.*"

Suddenly Robobutt listed steeply to one side.

Eleanor and Ned staggered backward.

Zack looked at the screen. But it was dark. "What's happening?" said Zack.

"Buttantula clinging to Robobutt's exterior," announced Robobutt.

"Full thrust!" commanded Ned.

Robobutt applied full thrust.

Despite the buttantula's deadly embrace, Robobutt continued to rise into the sky, although more slowly and unsteadily than before.

"Can't you get rid of it?" said Eleanor.

"I am doing my best," said Robobutt. "But this contingency was not programmed into my system."

"I would have thought that was true for pretty much everything on this whole mission." said Eleanor.

"You're right," said Ned, "but our best bet is to keep rising. When we get to a high enough altitude, the buttantula will simply freeze to death."

"If we don't get crushed to death on the way," said Zack's butt.

Ned shrugged. "Don't worry. Robobutt's outer shell is made of double-strength steel. She survived a twin tyrannosore-arse attack. I don't think a buttantula — even one this big — is going to pose too much of a threat."

"Oh yeah?" said Eleanor, "then how do you explain that?"

There was a loud groaning noise. The walls of the control room were starting to warp and buckle.

"Buttantula crushing Robobutt," announced Robobutt matter-of-factly. "Robobutt losing altitude."

Zack could feel his stomach somewhere up around his throat.

Eleanor was right.

Things were not okay.

In fact, things could hardly get much worse.

They were dropping.

Fast.

And the walls were closing in.

CHAPTER FIFTY-THREE

Crush!

Robobutt hit the ground with a sickening crunch.

Zack was thrown to the floor.

He looked up at the ceiling.

There were two large bulges. And they were getting bigger.

Zack screamed.

It could only mean one thing.

Or, rather, *two* things.

The buttantula's fangs!

Zack's mouth went dry.

If those fangs broke through, the amount of venom that would be released into the cabin would be nothing less than torrential.

And if they weren't drowned in the buttantula's venom, they could look forward to being crushed to death by its powerful legs.

And if they were really lucky, Zack figured, maybe both would happen at the same time.

At least they wouldn't suffer much, he thought. But that was a small consolation. The hardest part was waiting.

"Warning! Warning!" announced Robobutt. "Buttantula biting and crushing Robobutt. Repeat. Buttantula biting and crushing Robobutt!"

"Yeah, I think we get the picture, thanks," said Ned gloomily as his greatest creation crumbled around him.

"Warning! Warning!" said Robobutt.

"We *know!*" said Ned.

"No," said Robobutt. "A *new* warning. Great White Butt approaching!"

"Great!" said Eleanor. "This day just keeps getting better and better. I expect the entire univarse will blow up any second . . . well, we can only hope."

Zack gulped. Eleanor's sarcasm was the last thing he — or anyone else — needed. Rivets were popping and falling around them. The fang points in the ceiling were becoming more and more clearly defined. Robobutt was helpless against the buttantula, and now the Great White Butt was here to finish them off.

The noise of the buckling metal was deafening.

Zack braced himself.

His butt braced itself.

Eleanor braced herself.

Ned braced himself.

The Mutant Maggot Lord tried his best to brace what little self there was left of him to brace.

And then . . .

CHAPTER FIFTY-FOUR

Nothing

. . . nothing.

CHAPTER FIFTY-FIVE

Gift

Well, nothing *bad,* at least.

The noise stopped.

The butt-fighters opened their eyes. They held their breath.

The roof stopped bulging.

Nobody dared to exhale in case the nightmare began again.

But it didn't.

In fact, things got even better.

The buttantula's legs released their grip on the outside of Robobutt and disappeared, revealing a sight so extraordinary and so unexpected that the butt-fighters wondered if they were suffering a collective delusion brought on by methane madness.

The Great White Butt was rescuing them!

He had pried the buttantula's powerful legs off

Robobutt and was now pulverizing and pummeling the hapless buttantula into the ground.

"Great White Butt destroying buttantula," reported Robobutt, quickly recovering from the near-fatal embrace.

"He will be destroying us next if we don't get out of here fast," said Eleanor. "Let's go!"

"But the Great White Butt is my friend," said Robobutt. "He saved me."

"He is not your friend," spat Eleanor. "Or anybody else's friend. He is the most evil butt in history!"

"Who you didn't want to kill when you had the chance," said Zack.

"Who you *couldn't* kill when you had the chance," said Eleanor.

"Who at least I *tried* to kill when I had the chance," said Zack.

"Can you still fly, Robobutt?" said Eleanor.

"I do not know," said Robobutt. "I am creating a damage report now."

"Oh, gross," said Zack's butt. "Look at that!"

Out the window they could see that the Great White Butt was pulling the buttantula's legs off one by one.

"He is such a bully!" said Zack's butt.

"Poor thing," said the Mutant Maggot Lord. "I can sympathize. I know how much that hurts."

Eleanor whipped around to face him. In all the excitement she'd forgotten about him being there. "Who — *and what* — are you, anyway?" she said.

"Ah, have you forgotten me so soon?" said the Mutant

Maggot Lord. "I, who sacrificed my life, so that you could live?"

Eleanor stared at him with wide eyes. "Kisser?" she said. "Is that you?"

"I *used* to be the Kisser," said the Mutant Maggot Lord. "But that was another lifetime ago. A couple, in fact. I'm somebody else now."

"It's the Mutant Maggot Lord," said Zack.

Eleanor regarded him with a mixture of suspicion, pity, and disgust. "But I thought you were eaten by the mutant zombie maggots!" she said.

"I was," said the Mutant Maggot Lord. "It was a *very* unpleasant experience."

"But shouldn't you be dead?" said Eleanor, frowning.

"I was close enough to it," said the Mutant Maggot Lord. "For a little while, at least. But then the mutant zombie maggots turned into mutant zombie blowflies and I reconstituted myself from their puke."

"You just don't give up, do you?" said Eleanor. "I guess we should really call you the Mutant Zombie Blowfly Barf Lord."

"The *Mutant* Mutant Zombie Blowfly Barf Lord, to be completely accurate," said Ned coldly. "But we'll just call you "the Mutant Barf Lord" to keep things simple."

"I guess you're still angry about when I tried to kill you back in the Great Windy Dessert," said the Mutant Barf Lord. "But I really am sorry."

"Angry?" said Ned. "Me? Angry?" He was silent as he searched unsuccessfully for words to express exactly how angry he was. "Apology *not* accepted!" he finally blurted before turning away.

"I understand," said the Mutant Barf Lord. "But I really have changed. Honestly! I was confused back then. But now I'm on your side. I want to help you."

"Oh, gross!" said Zack's butt. "I think I'm going to be sick."

"That's no way to speak to a guest," said Zack. "Even if he *is* going to make you sick."

"I'm not talking about the Mutant Barf Lord," said Zack's butt, pointing at the screen.

Zack looked up.

And gasped.

The Great White Butt was approaching Robobutt with the still-quivering buttantula abdomen in his arms.

"Oh no!" said Eleanor. "He's coming! Liftoff, Robobutt!"

"Damage report not yet complete," said Robobutt.

"You'll have a lot more damage to report if you don't take off now!" said Eleanor. "We'll be smashed to pieces!"

"I don't think so," said Ned.

"What do you mean, you don't *think* so?" said Eleanor. "You saw what he just did to the buttantula."

"Look closely," said Ned. "The Great White Butt appears to be offering the buttantula cheeks to Robobutt. If I didn't know better, I'd say . . ."

He hesitated.

"What?" said Zack, not daring to take his eyes off the Great White Butt, who was kneeling in front of them, holding the legless buttantula in his outstretched hands.

"Well," said Ned, "it sounds crazy, but if I didn't know better, I'd say the Great White Butt is offering Robobutt a gift."

CHAPTER FIFTY-SIX

Proposal

The butt-fighters stared at the Great White Butt. They weren't used to seeing him behaving so politely.

"But *why*?" said Eleanor. "Why is he giving Robobutt a present?"

"Robobutt *is* a very good-looking butt," said Ned, "even if I do say so myself."

"You mean," said Eleanor, dumbfounded, "the Great White Butt doesn't realize Robobutt is just a machine? He thinks she's real?"

"Apparently so," said Ned.

"We thought she was real at first, too, don't forget," said Zack.

"Yes, but we're humans," said Eleanor, "not butts."

"Speak for yourself," said Zack's butt. "*I* thought she was real."

Eleanor shot it a dangerous look. "I'm still not speaking to you. Not now. Not ever."

Before Zack's butt could respond, Robobutt interrupted. "Request permission to accept gift from Great White Butt."

"Permission granted," said Ned, clearly pleased that his robotic butt was so convincing that she had fooled the Great White Butt himself. "It wouldn't do to offend our new best friend, now, would it?"

Robobutt stretched out her arms and received the pulsating prize in her hands. "Thank you."

"It is my pleasure to serve you," rumbled the Great White Butt, his voice — but thankfully not the *smell* of his voice — being broadcast via the external microphone located in one of Robobutt's fake pimples. "This buttantula will not bother you again, and its juices make a very fine perfume, which will only enhance your loveliness."

"Wow," said Eleanor. "What a charmer! Who would have guessed?"

The Mutant Barf Lord drew in his breath to speak, but was cut short by Ned.

"Shush!" said Ned. "We can't afford for the Great White Butt to get suspicious."

"But he can't hear us, can he?" said Zack.

"He shouldn't be able to," said Ned, "but after what Robobutt's been through, we'd better be careful. There may be some gaps where sound can get through. Robobutt, use your inside voice on the lowest possible setting."

"Affirmative," whispered Robobutt.

"I trust the buttantula did not cause you too much distress," said the Great White Butt.

Robobutt considered the Great White Butt's inquiry. "Negative," she said, switching back to her outside voice. "Damage report indicates minor malfunctions in control and navigation systems and moderate buckling of left outer cheek, but otherwise I am ninety percent operational."

Ned winced. "Too much Robospeak," he whispered to Robobutt. "Switch to casual mode."

"Affirmative," whispered Robobutt. "Oops, I mean, okay!"

But the Great White Butt didn't seem to notice or worry about Robobutt's lapse. "Why are you not at the Crack of Doom with the others?" he said. "We are leaving very soon!"

"What should I say?" whispered Robobutt, internally.

"Ask for more information!" said Ned.

"Leaving?" said Robobutt. "Where to?"

"You weren't at last night's meeting, were you?" said the Great White Butt. "I'm sure I would remember seeing a butt as lovely as you."

"No," said Robobutt. "I was on my way but I got stuck in the buttantula's web."

"Of course," said the Great White Butt. "Forgive me, but there is so much to do. The Earth will soon be struck by a devastating arseteroid. It will wipe out all buttosaur life on the Earth. Look into the sky. You can already see the glow."

Robobutt looked up, giving the butt-fighters a clear view of a tiny but bright point of light in the sky.

"Oh my goodness," said Robobutt. "That's terrible!"

"Yes," said the Great White Butt. "But don't worry. I have a plan for the complete evacuation of all Great White Buttosaurs from the planet."

"That's what *you* think," said Zack.

"Shush!" said the Mutant Barf Lord. "We can't afford to miss anything!"

"In less than two hours every Great White Buttosaur on Earth will travel to the arseteroid-free future by means of a brown hole time gate," continued the Great White Butt. "Once there, we will create a new world. A world of Great White Butts. I shall be their king, naturally. But what is a king without his queen? I have traveled across time and space and have never met a Great White Butt as great or as white or as beautiful as you. What do you say? Will you consent to be my bride, my wife, and my queen, to rule alongside me over the greatest Great White Butt empire the univarse has ever known?"

The butt-fighters were flabbergasted.

They'd all learned to expect the unexpected from the Great White Butt, but none of them had expected this.

The Great White Butt was in love.

With Robobutt!

CHAPTER FIFTY-SEVEN

Stalling

The butt-fighters had known about the Great White Butt's plan for evacuation, of course, but they hadn't imagined in their wildest dreams that he would fall in love with Robobutt. And judging by Robobutt's silence, it was clear that neither had she.

"The Great White Butt's request falls outside mission protocols," Robobutt finally said to Ned. "Request suggestion for appropriate response."

"Tell him you need some time to think," said Ned.

"Time to think about what?!" said Eleanor. "Are you out of your mind? Robobutt can't get married. Especially not to the Great White Butt."

"Calm down, Eleanor," said Zack. "This might be just the break we need."

"Zack could be right," said Ned. "It can't hurt to think this through properly. Go ahead, Robobutt."

"Thank you, Great White Butt, for your kind offer,"

said Robobutt. "I am honored, and flattered, of course. But it is such a big decision to make so quickly. Do you mind if I have a few moments alone to think about it?"

"What is there to think about?" said the Great White Butt. "You won't find a butt greater or whiter than me! And certainly not in the time remaining on this planet."

"I know," said Robobutt. "But it's all very sudden, and I'd just like to be sure, that's all."

"I understand," said the Great White Butt. "But we don't have much time. I shall return in five minutes for your answer."

"Thank you," said Robobutt.

The butt-fighters watched the Great White Butt walk toward the canyon and stand with his back turned to them.

"Well?" said Ned. "What do you think?"

"I say we play for time," said Zack. "The longer we can stall and keep the Great White Butt here, the more likely it is that the arseteroid will hit before he can begin the evacuation."

"Good plan," said Ned. "What do you think, Eleanor?"

"I've got a better idea," she replied quickly. "We've got the Great White Butt in front of us. On the edge of a canyon. Unsuspecting and completely helpless. I say we fire Robobutt's nuclear wart-head and blast him right over the edge. By the time the Great White Butt realizes what's happened, he will be splattered all over the rocks at the bottom and he will never trouble us — or the universe — ever again."

Ned nodded. "That sounds like a good plan too."

"I don't think so," said the Mutant Barf Lord.

"Nobody asked you," said Eleanor.

"Eleanor, I understand your attitude," said the Mutant Barf Lord. "But as I sacrificed my life for you — and the cause — I think I have the right to at least be heard."

"He does have a point," said Zack.

Eleanor glared at Zack. Then she glared at the Mutant Barf Lord. "Whatever," she shrugged.

"Thank you," said the Mutant Barf Lord, the fingers on his remaining arm trembling slightly. "I merely wanted to make the point that violence has never worked against the Great White Butt. We all know he is a freak. He's survived a buttcano blast and an interplanetary head-on collision. I tell you, the Great White Butt is indestructible and if you think that a mere fall into a canyon will finish him off, you could be throwing away the best chance we've ever had of ridding the univarse of this menace once and for all."

"Which is?" said Eleanor.

"Play for time, as Zack suggests," said the Mutant Barf Lord. "But don't stay here. Go back with him to the Crack of Doom and make sure he is directly underneath the arseteroid when it hits. Use the nuclear wart-head to immobilize him, by all means, but don't rely on it to destroy him. Let the arseteroid take care of him. This is an arseteroid — you will remember — that is responsible for one of the greatest mass extinctions of all time. If that doesn't finish him off then nothing will. But at least we will have given it our best possible shot. Anything less would be doing a disservice to what is — whether you like to admit it or not — a very worthy adversary."

Eleanor shook her head. "There's nothing *worthy* about the Great White Butt," she said. "I don't care how indestructible he is or if he does give legless buttantula abdomens to his girlfriends. There's not a single redeeming bone in his horrible detestable flabby cheeks."

"Butts don't have *any* bones," said Zack's butt.

"Shut up!" said Eleanor. "I'm *still* not speaking to you."

"I think the Mutant Barf Lord has a good point, though," said Zack. "Remember how our attempt to destroy the newborn Great White Butt backfired?"

"*Your* attempt," she said. "A Great White Butt in the hand is worth millions of Great White Butts at the Crack of Doom. I say we nuclear wart-head him into oblivion right now. While we still can."

"They are all good plans," said Ned. "But much as it pains me to say it, I agree with the Mutant Barf Lord. It's the only absolutely guaranteed way we have of destroying the Great White Butt — not just for now, but for all time."

"I agree," said Zack.

"Me too," said Zack's butt.

"Looks like I'm outvoted," said Eleanor. "I just hope you all know what you're doing."

CHAPTER FIFTY-EIGHT

Kiss

The Great White Butt turned and walked back toward Robobutt. "So, my dear, what is your decision?" he said. "Will you be my bride?"

"What should I tell him?" said Robobutt, internally.

"Accept," said Eleanor, "but insist on a wedding *before* you leave."

"Good thinking, Eleanor!" said Ned.

"I accept your offer of marriage," said Robobutt. "But my honor requires that we marry before we depart for our new kingdom."

"But," said the Great White Butt, "a Great White Butt as beautiful — and rare — as you should have a ceremony fit for a queen. I suggest we get married in the new world when there will be more time to have the sort of wedding you deserve. A beautiful wedding gown made out of the softest, whitest toilet paper in the world, a giant fluffy pink toilet seat cover for your throne, and a bouquet made out of human heads . . ."

"No," said Robobutt. "I may be a little old-fashioned, but as a single female it wouldn't be right for me to travel alone with you. If we can't be married first then I must refuse."

At this the Great White Butt visibly softened.

"But of course," he said. "If that is your wish then that is how it shall be. I have spent a lifetime searching for you — I'm not going to let a small detail like this come between us."

As the Great White Butt spoke he was leaning in closer and closer to Robobutt.

"He'll squash the buttantula if he's not careful," said Ned.

"Is he about to do what I think he's about to do?" said Eleanor.

"What?" said Zack's butt.

"He's going to kiss us!" said Eleanor, her eyes wide.

"Gross!" said Zack's butt, covering its eye with both hands.

But the Great White Butt's cheeks had barely touched Robobutt's cheeks when the ground began to shake in a series of violent tremors.

"What's that?" said Zack.

An earsplitting bellow followed by a series of loud pounding noises disturbed the romantic atmosphere.

"Uh-oh," said Ned. "Looks like Romeo's got some competition."

Zack stared at the awesome creature stomping heavily along the canyon edge toward them.

It was the biggest, chunkiest, most muscle-bound butt Zack had ever seen. And definitely the ugliest. It was covered in thick black bristly hair, except for a bare leathery patch of skin on each cheek. The hairy beast was beating on these patches with its huge fists and bellowing ferociously.

"Oh no," said the Great White Butt, pulling away from Robobutt. "Not this *bozo*. Not *now*!"

CHAPTER FIFTY-NINE

Stink Kong

Who is it?" said Robobutt, who had no matching files to help her recognize this terrifying buttosaur.

"Stink Kong!" said the Great White Butt. "My old enemy. Look how the cocobutt-trees wither and die as he approaches. He should be ashamed of himself! What a disgusting pig!"

"That's rich, coming from him," whispered Eleanor. "But then I guess it takes one to know one."

"I'm sorry, my love," said the Great White Butt apologetically to Robobutt. "I'm going to have to take care of this ugly ape once and for all. Things could get a little rough. You might want to stand aside and cover your eye."

"Whatever you say," said Robobutt. "Good luck!"

Robobutt reversed as far as she could and drew her hand up across the buttcam concealed on her roof.

"No!" said Ned. "Don't do that! We want to watch!"

Robobutt obediently parted her fingers.

The fight was already in full swing.

Stink Kong was pounding the Great White Butt like a punching bag. The Great White Butt grabbed Stink Kong in a death-hug and threw him to the ground.

Zack could feel the ground shake, even through Robobutt. "Why doesn't he just gas Stink Kong and get it over with?" said Zack.

"That only works on animals and humans," said Zack's butt. "We don't have noses, remember?"

"But what about Stenchgantor?" said Zack. "It had a nose. I defeated it with a pair of dirty socks!"

"All right, all right, enough already about how you defeated Stenchgantor with your dirty socks," said Eleanor. "It was a great achievement, but do you have to go on about it?"

"You're just jealous," said Zack.

"Yeah, right," said Eleanor. "Jealous of your total lack of personal hygiene. I guess I can only dream of having feet — or a butt — as smelly as yours."

"Hey!" said Zack's butt. "That's out of line."

"Yeah?" said Eleanor. "What are you going to do about it?"

Zack's butt bent over and was about to zap Eleanor when there was a huge earth-shattering crash.

Zack looked up to see the Great White Butt lying on his back and Stink Kong jumping up and down on him as if he were a trampoline.

"That Stink Kong sure has some moves," said Ned.

"But I don't think that using the Great White Butt as a trampoline is such a good idea."

Suddenly Stink Kong was blown high into the air by a giant brown geyser emitted from the center of the Great White Butt.

"That's why I didn't think it was a good idea," said Ned.

Zack heard a hissing sound behind him.

He turned and saw the Mutant Barf Lord totally engrossed in the fight, punching the air with his remaining arm and hissing "Yesss!"

Then, without warning, Robobutt began to rise into the air.

"Robobutt?" said Ned. "What are you doing? I didn't tell you to lift off!"

"Negative," said Robobutt. "Robobutt is not lifting off. Robobutt is being carried away by a large buttodactyl."

"Oh, great!" said Ned. "*Buttodactyls.* That's all we need!"

CHAPTER SIXTY

Buttodactyl

Within moments Stink Kong and the Great White Butt were just tiny figures sparring on the far side of the canyon a long, long way beneath them.

"Activate thrusters, Robobutt!" said Ned.

"Negative," said Robobutt. "Thrusters are not responding."

"Turbo-assisted jet repulsion unit!" yelled Ned.

"Negative," said Robobutt. "Turbo-assisted jet repulsion unit damaged by the buttantula."

"Have you got anything?" said Ned through gritted teeth. "Anything at all?"

"Of course," said Robobutt. "I have onboard tea- and coffee-making facilities. Would you like milk with that, madam? Sugar? One lump or two thousand? Yes, it is a very nice day. I am Robobutt. Ro-bo-butt. RO. BO. BUTT. WITH. MILK."

"What's going on, Ned?" said Zack. "What's wrong with Robobutt?"

"Poor old girl, she's been knocked around a bit too much," said Ned. "Sounds like her higher speech and thinking functions have been scrambled, and her thrusters and turbo are out of action."

"Is there anything we can do?" said Eleanor, staring at the buttcam image of the buttodactyl's leathery cheek-wings as they pushed down on either side of the screen.

"I don't think so," said Ned, studying his *What Buttosaur Is That?* book. "Buttodactyls are powerful. Says here an adult buttodactyl can have a wingspan of up to one hundred fifty feet. Its wings are made of a membrane that stretches from its fingers to its back legs. And they're methane assisted!"

"A brilliant design!" hissed the Mutant Barf Lord.

"When we want the opinion of a mutant we'll ask for it," said Eleanor coldly.

"Some of them are toothless," said Ned, still reading from his book, "while others have hundreds of bristle-like teeth lining their long, razor-sharp beaks. . . ."

"Ned," said Eleanor. "Thanks for the lecture. It's truly fascinating. But what I want to know is can we fire something at it?"

"I'm afraid not," said Ned. "The buttodactyl is directly above us. There is no artillery in the roof."

"It doesn't matter," said the Mutant Barf Lord. "I wouldn't give up on the Great White Butt yet. He won't abandon Robobutt that easily. He'll save us."

"You sound like you're on his side," said Eleanor suspiciously.

The Mutant Barf Lord laughed. "Once upon a time," he said. "But no more. Anybody can make a mistake."

Eleanor stared at the sad heap of flesh and sticks and leaves in front of her.

"Body?" she said. "You call that a *body*?"

Zack groaned. "Uh-oh," he said. "That doesn't look good."

"You're telling me," said Eleanor.

"No," said Zack. "Look at the screen."

Eleanor looked at the screen. They were flying toward an enormous buttcano. The buttcano was ringed by an impressive collar of sheer black stone rising many thousands of feet straight up. It made the Great White Butt's buttcano look like an anthill.

As they drew closer, the butt-fighters could see buttodactyl nests wedged in among the ledges of the rock face.

And, even more worryingly, they could see the heads of hungry buttodactyl chicks eagerly poking out of the nests, opening and closing their razor-edged cheeks.

"I never thought I'd hear myself saying this," said Zack, "but I hope the Great White Butt gets here soon."

CHAPTER SIXTY ONE

Nest

The buttodactyl flew up the face of the buttcano. It flew until it had almost reached the highest point, where the rock met the smoking mouth of the vent. There, in a nest so large that it looked like it was constructed out of tree trunks, were more buttodactyl chicks.

Three of them — each a rusty red color. And each with a razor-sharp beak.

They were so excited by the arrival of their meal that they were practically leaping out of the nest.

"So, what's our plan?" said Zack.

Ned laughed without humor. "Plan? That assumes that we knew this was going to happen. I'm not too worried about the chicks. I doubt they'll be able to do much damage to Robobutt's exterior. . . ."

"Famous last words," said Eleanor. "That's what you said about the buttantula, and look what happened."

"True, Eleanor," said Ned. "I'm doing my best. This isn't easy for anybody, you know. We're all in uncharted territory here."

"I'm sorry," said Eleanor, biting her fingernail. "I guess the thought of becoming a buttodactyl snack has got me a little tense."

"I don't think you're going to have to worry about that," said Zack's butt as the buttodactyl placed Robobutt down on a ledge a short distance above the nest. "At least not for a little while."

"So, we're not going to be eaten?" said Zack.

"Not yet," said Ned. "Looks like they're starting with an appetizer."

Eleanor peered at the image of the nest on buttcam . . . and screamed. The buttodactyl that had brought them there was dangling a small pink butt above her babies' beaks.

"Aaaggghh!" screamed the helpless butt.

"That's my butt!" yelled Eleanor, leaping to her feet. "I've got to save it!"

"Don't be a fool!" said Zack.

"Look who's talking," said Eleanor. "You'd save your butt if it was down there, wouldn't you?"

Zack looked at the wildly snapping beaks of the buttodactyls and hesitated.

"Well?" said his butt. "Wouldn't you?"

Zack looked at his butt. And then back at the buttodactyls. And then back at his butt. "I suppose so," said Zack, uncertainly. "But those things will eat you alive!"

"Better that than knowing I didn't try to save my butt

when I had the chance," said Eleanor, already standing in the teleport beam.

Zack sighed. "Hang on," he said. "I'll come with you."

"Be careful, Zack," said his butt.

"Of course," said Zack. " 'Careful' is my middle name."

"No, it's not," said his butt. "It's Henry."

"Shush," said Zack. "I thought I told you never to say that ever again."

"Sorry, Zack," said his butt. "Your secret's safe with me."

"And me," said Eleanor.

"And me," smirked Ned.

"And me," said the Mutant Barf Lord, making a sound somewhere between laughter and throwing up. But whatever sound it was, Zack Henry Freeman didn't like it.

CHAPTER SIXTY-TWO

Snatch!

Zack and Eleanor teleported onto the ledge of the buttcano.

The buttodactyl nest was about thirty feet below them.

Eleanor pulled a roll of triple-strength toilet paper from her butt-fighter utility belt.

She wrapped a length around her waist and knotted it tightly. She then handed the roll to Zack. "Let it out slowly," she yelled against the roar of the wind, "and get a good grip on the rock face. You may have to take my whole weight."

"Okay!" yelled Zack. "Be careful."

"No time for that," called Eleanor as she launched herself backward over the ledge and rappelled down a narrow crevice. The buttodactyl was perched on the edge of the nest with its back to her. It had Eleanor's butt in its beak, but seemed unable to decide which of the screaming chicks to give the prize to.

Zack bit his lip.

It was scary up on the ledge.

In the sky above him he could see the menacing glow of the approaching arseteroid. It was noticeably bigger now and getting larger by the second.

And down below — way down below — he could see a prehistoric stink bog.

The sight made him shiver.

Stink bogs were a one-way trip to fossil museums of the future. That's if there *was* a future for fossil museums to exist in, thought Zack grimly.

Once a buttosaur — or a person for that matter — got stuck in a stink bog, that was it. The rotting matter was so thick and sticky that nothing could escape it. With great difficulty, Zack tore his gaze — and his thoughts — away from the stink bog and looked down to check on Eleanor's progress.

She was almost three-quarters of the way down the crevice to the nest. But then the buttodactyl looked back and noticed her.

Out of sheer surprise it opened its beak and dropped Eleanor's butt, which fell into the beak of the closest chick. The mother squawked a loud warning rasp at Eleanor.

"That's exactly how I feel about you too," said Eleanor as she leaped from the wall and swung — Tarzan style — over the top of the nest. Reaching down as she swept past, she plucked her butt out of the buttodactyl chick's beak. Then she swung upward into the sky.

"Eleanor?" said her butt, who was dazed and almost blue from the cold.

"Don't worry," said Eleanor, hugging her butt to her chest. "I've got you. And I'm not letting go . . . whether you like it or not!"

"I like it . . . ," said her butt, as Eleanor reached the furthermost point of her swing.

But their ordeal was not over yet.

They now had to swing back through a gauntlet of enraged buttodactyl chicks and their super-enraged buttodactyl mother.

Eleanor took a deep breath, gripped the toilet paper extra hard, and let out a banshee scream that her father had taught her.

The buttodactyls were too stunned to snap at her as she swooped past.

"Great going, Eleanor," said her butt.

"Thanks," said Eleanor as she gripped the rock face and, helped by her butt, began climbing back up to the ledge.

CHAPTER SIXTY-THREE

Panic

Zack hauled in the toilet paper as fast as he could.
He was looking out straight ahead of him —- trying not to look down — when he saw a familiar shape flying through the air toward them.

The Great White Butt!

"Hurry, Eleanor!" yelled Zack.

"What do you think I'm doing?" she said. "I'm going as fast as I can."

"Look behind you," said Zack.

Eleanor glanced over her shoulder. She knew as well as Zack that it would be disastrous for the Great White Butt to catch them out here. If he realized that Robobutt was a machine, their whole plan would come unraveled in an instant.

Zack was really sweating now.

The Great White Butt was getting closer.

And to make things worse, the mother buttodactyl

was heading their way to retrieve the butt that had been stolen from her.

The fossil museum of the future was looking more and more like a real possibility with every passing second.

Zack imagined his bones being excavated from the stink bog.

The bones would be labeled and put into a glass case.

Maybe they'd even be assembled and motorized and hooked up to a button on the outside of the case for snotty schoolkids to push and laugh at as his bones jiggled around.

The buttodactyl was swooping and snapping at the toilet paper. One of the perforations began to tear apart.

"Faster!" yelled Zack, grimacing as he strained to pull Eleanor up the mountain. "The Great White Butt is almost here!"

Suddenly Eleanor's butt appeared . . . and then Eleanor's head.

She reached up and Zack pulled them both onto the ledge beside him, almost crying with relief.

"Come on," he said, "let's get back into Robobutt while we still have time."

They clambered up and into Robobutt's teleportation beam.

The buttodactyl swooped in for a final desperate attempt to retrieve Eleanor's butt. This time Eleanor's butt joined Eleanor in a banshee scream that scared the buttodactyl stiff and sent the unfortunate creature plummeting over the ledge and down toward the stink bog below.

But despite whatever humiliating fate was in store for it in the future, it received no sympathy from the butt-fighters, who were already teleporting back to the relative safety of Robobutt.

Or so they thought.

CHAPTER SIXTY-FOUR

Skullduggery

As Zack rematerialized inside Robobutt, he could tell something was wrong. Exactly what, however, he couldn't quite put his finger on.

Was it the fact that Ned was lying face down in a pool of blood?

Or was it the fact that the Mutant Barf Lord was sitting in a chair with a butt-gun pointed at them?

Zack thought quickly — well, as quickly as you can in the midst of a state of total confusion — and came to the conclusion that it was both of these things put together.

Something was most definitely — and most horribly — wrong. As wrong as something most definitely and most horribly wrong could possibly be.

"Welcome back," said the Mutant Barf Lord. "But I'm afraid there's been a little accident."

"What have you done, you putrid piece of slime?" said Eleanor, staring in shock at Ned's body.

"Well," said the Mutant Barf Lord, "there was a slight difference of opinion between myself and Ned while you were out and . . ."

"You *shot* Ned!" said Eleanor.

"*Shot* is a very strong word," said the Mutant Barf Lord.

"But it's the *right* word," said Eleanor.

"I had no choice," said the Mutant Barf Lord. "He was threatening the success of the mission!"

"Ned *was* the mission!" yelled Zack, blinking back tears. "He *built* Robobutt. He rescued us. If it wasn't for him none of us would even be here!"

"No," said the Mutant Barf Lord. "And if he'd had his way none of you would be here now. He wanted to just fly away and leave you."

"Ned would never do a thing like that," said Eleanor. "You haven't changed at all. You're still a liar. And a lousy one. And besides, if you're so interested in our welfare, why are you pointing a gun at us?"

The Mutant Barf Lord shifted uncomfortably. "Because I rather suspected that you wouldn't believe my side of the story and that you might try to do something silly."

"Why don't we ask Robobutt?" said Eleanor.

"I'm afraid that won't be possible," said the Mutant Barf Lord. "She is taking a little nap."

"We're under manual control?" said Zack.

"No, you fool," said the Mutant Barf Lord coldly. "You're under *my* control."

Zack looked into the Mutant Barf Lord's eyes. As the Kisser, the Mutant Barf Lord had switched allegiance from the butt-fighters to the butts. As the Mutant Maggot Lord, he'd switched allegiance from the butts to his beloved maggots and then finally back to the butt-fighters. Now it seemed he had switched allegiance once again.

Slowly, as Zack stared into the depths of the Mutant Barf Lord's vacant eyes, he realized the truth. The Mutant Barf Lord's true allegiance was to nobody but himself. He was interested only in power. *Absolute power.* And if that came at the cost of the survival of the human race, then that was a price the Mutant Barf Lord was willing to pay. Even his apparent selflessness in sacrificing himself to the mutant maggots was a purely selfish act: part of a desperate — but calculated — strategy to transform himself yet again in his endless, insatiable quest for power. Nothing — and nobody — else mattered. Not Ned, not Eleanor, not Zack, and not . . .

"Oh no!" said Zack. "Where's my butt? What have you done with my butt? I swear, if you've hurt it . . ."

Suddenly there was an almighty jolt as Robobutt rose into the air again.

But not under her own power.

While the butt-fighters had been discovering the truth about the Mutant Barf Lord, the Great White Butt had been busy smashing the unfortunate mother buttodactyl — which it had intercepted on its plunge into the stink bog — against the cliff face. Its broken body and splattered brains were being hungrily devoured by the buttodactyl chicks. And Robobutt was now cradled safely in the Great White Butt's arms.

"Sorry about that, my love," said the Great White Butt in a soothing voice as they took off. "But don't worry. Neither Stink Kong nor the buttodactyl will be giving us any further trouble. Soon we'll be at the Crack of Doom, where we'll be married and leave for our honeymoon, on the new Earth where we will live happily ever after."

CHAPTER SIXTY-FIVE

Destiny?

Meanwhile, on board Robobutt, the sudden movement had caused the butt-fighters to lose their footing and fall to the ground in a sprawling heap. Eleanor landed first. Her butt fell on top of her. Zack landed on top of it and then his butt fell on top of them all.

"Where did you come from?" said Zack, overjoyed to see his butt again.

"I was hiding in the roof," said his butt. "Hiding from *him*!" Zack's butt pointed at the Mutant Barf Lord, who, being more liquid than solid, hadn't been affected by the upheaval. "He went crazy! He killed Ned!"

"We know," said Zack, patting his butt.

"Ned was getting ready to fire Robobutt's nuclear wart-head at the Great White Butt," said Zack's butt.

"Why?" said Eleanor.

"To protect you and Zack," said Zack's butt. "He was

worried that the Great White Butt was going to see you. And then the Mutant Barf Lord went crazy. He grabbed a butt-gun and shot Ned in the back. Then he tried to kill me, but I ran away and hid."

"That sounds more like the Kisser that I've come to know and despise," said Eleanor grimly. "Just you wait. By the time I get through with you, you're going to wish you'd never reconstituted yourself. You're going to wish you'd never crawled out of the brown lake alive. In fact, you're going to wish that you'd never been born."

"I'm not sure that hurting me is such a good idea," said the Mutant Barf Lord. "Stop and *think* about it. You're a smart girl, Eleanor. Headstrong, but smart. No matter what you do to me — or *think* you want to do to me — the Great White Butt's rise is inevitable, and we have the perfect opportunity to take advantage of it."

"There's nothing 'inevitable' about the Great White Butt's rise," said Eleanor. "We can still stop him !"

"But why would you *want* to stop him?" said the Mutant Barf Lord. "Don't you see? This is what was prophesied in *The Book of Buttageddon!* I am doing nothing more than helping destiny to fulfill itself."

Eleanor spat. "There's no such thing as *destiny*," she said. "It's not a place or a foregone conclusion. We're making it up as we go along, and we can work toward a better world or a world of Buttageddon — it's our choice — *your* choice — *right now*!"

"But that's my point exactly," said the Mutant Barf Lord. "With the aid of Robobutt we can rule the world alongside the Great White Butt! That opportunity doesn't come along every day, you know. By defeating the Great

White Butt now, we ultimately lose — we become nobod-ies with no power — but if we help the Great White Butt we win — *we win the world*."

"You mutated piece of mutant zombie blowfly barf," said Eleanor, walking toward the Mutant Barf Lord with her hands outstretched. "Give me the gun. Your dirty double-crossing treachery ends here."

"You want to talk about dirty double-crossing treach-ery?" said the Mutant Barf Lord. "Let's start with you riding around in a robotic butt making promises of mar-riage that you have no intention of keeping! I would have thought that qualified as dirty double-crossing treachery on at least two counts: pretending to be what you are not and intended breach of promise."

Eleanor stared at the Mutant Barf Lord, her eyes cold. "I never said I was perfect."

"Neither did I," said the Mutant Barf Lord, raising the butt-gun.

"No, Eleanor!" said Zack. "Stop! He's deranged. He'll do it!"

"Zack's right," said the Mutant Barf Lord. "I will."

But Eleanor didn't say a word. She just continued walking toward him.

Zack saw the Mutant Barf Lord's finger twitch on the trigger.

There was a blast of light and an incredible noise as three rounds of atomic butt-blasting bullets leaped from the mouth of the gun.

CHAPTER SIXTY-SIX

Good-byes

E eergggh!" said a voice.

But it wasn't Eleanor.

It was her butt.

At the crucial moment it had leaped in front of the Mutant Barf Lord's butt-gun and was now rolling around on the ground clutching its cheeks.

Eleanor fixed the surprised Mutant Barf Lord with a look of deadly intent and tore the gun from his hand, raised it to her shoulder, and pointed it at his head. Or, at least, what passed for his head.

He shielded himself weakly with his remaining arm, or, at least, what passed for his remaining arm.

"You can mess with me all you like," said Eleanor, "but nobody messes with my butt! Say good-bye, mutant — if there's anyone mutated enough to care . . ."

"Negative," said Robobutt, crackling back to life. "I

have checked my data banks. There is no one *that* mutated."

"Thanks, Robobutt," said Zack, who had taken advantage of the commotion to reactivate Robobutt.

"Guess it's just not your lucky day," said Eleanor to the Mutant Barf Lord as she squeezed the trigger.

Zack closed his eyes.

CHAPTER SIXTY-SEVEN

Housekeeping

When Zack opened his eyes, he was amazed to see that nothing had changed.

The Mutant Barf Lord was still sitting in his chair.

Eleanor was still standing in front of him with the gun.

And a glance out the window indicated that they were still speeding toward the Crack of Doom.

"The Mutant Barf Lord is still alive," said Robobutt. "Status report indicates the Mutant Barf Lord's body density is a mere one percent — in other words, he is ninety-nine percent flesh-free. The bullets have passed through him with little impact."

"Wish you'd told me that before," said Eleanor.

"You didn't ask," said Robobutt.

"Okay," said Eleanor. "I'm asking now. How do we get rid of this piece of bulletproof slime?"

"Removal of onboard slime best achieved by activation of wet and dry suction unit located in hall closet," said Robobutt.

The Mutant Barf Lord looked horrified.

"No," he said. "You wouldn't. . . . Not the vacuum cleaner!"

"I'm afraid so," said Zack, retrieving the unit from the closet. "You leave us no choice."

Zack switched it on.

The high-pitched suction unit roared into life.

The Mutant Barf Lord cowered in terror and started to slide across the floor and into a crevice.

"Quick, Zack!" yelled Eleanor. "He's getting away!"

Zack just smiled and fixed a crevice attachment to the end of the hose.

The Mutant Barf Lord screamed. Or, at least, made a noise that might have passed for a scream if anyone had been able to hear it above the vacuum cleaner's roar.

Schluuurrrrpp!

Within a moment the Mutant Barf Lord had disappeared up the deadly nozzle — his watery flesh no match for the awesome power of the heavy-duty butt-fighting vacuum cleaner.

Eleanor looked at the ex-Mutant Barf Lord, now just a thin watery puddle of blood and rotting flesh in the bottom of the hard plastic vacuum cleaner body.

"Good work, Zack," said Eleanor.

Zack, who was staring at the brown mush, hoped she was right.

He could see one of the Mutant Barf Lord's eyeballs floating in the midst of the liquefied remains — and worse still, it was staring back at him.

Zack shivered and turned away.

He looked across to where Eleanor's butt lay and saw his butt jumping up and down on top of it.

"What do you think you're doing?" said Zack.

"Butt-to-butt resuscitation," said Zack's butt.

"No!" said Eleanor, rushing across the room. "You'll kill her!"

"She was *already* dead," said Zack's butt. "It's worth a try!"

Suddenly Eleanor's butt groaned.

Eleanor kneeled down beside the two butts. "She's alive?" she said to Zack's butt.

"Yes," said Zack's butt, hopping off.

"Thank you," said Eleanor. "I'll take over now."

Zack's butt nodded gravely and stepped back.

Eleanor picked up her wounded butt and cradled it gently in her arms. "How are you feeling?" she said.

"Just a flesh wound," said her butt. "I developed a pretty thick hide out there in the jungle. I had to. I've suffered worse."

"You saved my life," said Eleanor.

"You saved mine," said Eleanor's butt. "It was the least I could do."

Eleanor bit her lip. "I'm really sorry," she said. "The last few years must have been very hard for you. I don't know how I'll ever make it up to you."

"It's okay," said her butt. "You just did."

CHAPTER SIXTY-EIGHT

Farewell

The mood inside Robobutt was somber as Zack and his butt dragged Ned Smelly's body to the area underneath the teleportation beam. Zack folded Ned's arms across his chest and placed his homemade metal helmet on his head.

"Ned was one of the best," said Zack. "Without him none of this would have been possible."

Tears came to Zack's eyes as he thought about how much they owed Ned. It was Ned who had rescued them from certain death after their crash landing in the Great Windy Desert. And it was Ned who had rescued them from the Kisser's treachery on the buttcano. And, of course, more recently, it was Ned who had rescued them from Buttageddon.

"He was a good man," said Eleanor, looking up from her butt. "I never heard him say a bad thing about anybody."

"Or any *butt*," said Zack's butt. "He was always kind to me. Even though he was a butt-fighter he was always kind."

"He was the best inventor a robotic butt could have wanted," said Robobutt quietly.

Zack stepped back with his head bowed. "May your butt be with you," he said solemnly. "Okay, Robobutt . . . take him up."

Robobutt's teleportation beam glowed, and Ned's body began to grow faint.

Suddenly Zack ran to the other side of the room. "Hang on, Robobutt!"

Zack returned with Ned's *What Buttosaur Is That?* and placed it on top of his almost transparent body. "I think he'd appreciate that," said Zack.

"So do I," said Robobutt.

CHAPTER SIXTY-NINE

Crack

Nobody spoke much as the Great White Butt carried them toward the Crack of Doom. The only sounds were the small whimpers of pain from Eleanor's butt as Eleanor dabbed at its wounds with cotton wool soaked in antiseptic.

"I'm sorry," said Eleanor, after each dab. "I'm sorry."

"It's all right," said Eleanor's butt. "I know you don't mean to hurt me."

Zack's butt wiped a tear from its eye and joined Zack, who was gazing at the buttcam screen.

Together they watched as the Great White Butt descended toward an enormous jagged smoking gash in the ground. They felt like they were looking directly down into the very bowels of the earth.

It was not a pretty sight.

Suddenly Zack's thoughts flashed back to his traumatic experiences inside the buttcano.

The brown lake.

The maggots.

The Great White Butt.

The match.

The gas.

The death stink.

The explosion.

But this was worse.

The sheer enormity of the Crack of Doom made the brown lake look like a harmless puddle.

The Great White Butt set Robobutt down gently.

"Destination reached," said Robobutt. "Prepare for wedding ceremony."

Zack and Eleanor looked across the room at each other. In a desperate mission already packed with danger, they both knew that this was the most dangerous part of all.

They looked at the screen.

And gasped.

Giant brown blobs were flying in all directions.

They were surrounded by thousands of Great White Butts.

Hundreds of thousands of Great White Butts.

Hundreds of thousands of Great White Butts involved in a free-for-all riot.

Somehow Robobutt — no matter how technologically advanced — didn't seem like much protection against an entire colony of Great White Butts.

CHAPTER SEVENTY

Tears

H ere we are," said the Great White Butt. "The Crack of Doom. My home. My subjects. Your subjects-to-be."

As the Great White Butt said this, all the Great White Butts immediately stopped their fighting and turned to their master. A ripple of excitement ran through the crowd.

"As you already know, our departure time is soon — very soon — but first I have an announcement," said the Great White Butt. "After a lifetime of searching for a butt as great and as white as myself I have finally found her. She is to be my wife and your queen. A fitting way to start our new world order!"

There was a roar of approval from the butts.

"Come, my bride," said the Great White Butt. "Give me your hand. It is time for us to be married."

Robobutt obediently extended her hand.

"What do you think we should do?" said Eleanor. "Should we detonate the nuclear wart-head?"

"No," said Zack. "It's still too early. We have to slow things down. If the marriage happens too quickly they'll leave before the arseteroid hits. We have to stall for as long as possible until it's too late for the butts to evacuate. We need to make sure the Great White Butt is underneath that arseteroid."

"How do I do this?" said Robobutt using her inside voice.

"Tell him you can't get married without a dress," said Eleanor's butt.

"Great idea," said Eleanor. "And flowers!"

"And music!" said Zack's butt.

Robobutt turned to the Great White Butt. "I'm really very excited about getting married," she said sweetly. "But I need a dress. And flowers. And music."

"But, my dear," said the Great White Butt, flushing crimson with impatience. "We must get married now. Dresses and flowers and music . . . these things take time to prepare. Time that we can barely afford, my darling. We must be off the planet before the arseteroid strikes. There is less time than you think."

Suddenly the butt-fighters were thrown to the ground as huge tremors shook Robobutt.

"What's happening?" said Zack, desperately trying to find something to grab on to.

"I don't know," said Eleanor. "If I didn't know that Robobutt was just a machine I'd say she was . . . she was *crying*."

"Crying?" said Zack. "But that's impossible. She can't . . . unless . . . hang on . . . that's brilliant!"

"What?" said Eleanor. "What's brillant?"

"Listen!" said Zack. "She's *pretending*."

"Don't cry, my sweet," said the Great White Butt, patting Robobutt gently. "Please don't cry. Of course you shall have these things. Anything you desire will be yours. A beautiful dress. The best flowers that have evolved so far, and music so sweet you'll think it was blown from the cheeks of the butt-angels themselves."

The Great White Butts stood motionless, staring at the sight of their queen-to-be sobbing.

"Well?" said the Great White Butt to his subjects. "What are you oafs waiting for?" He pointed at three butts. "You, you, and you! Get my queen a dress, flowers, and music. Hop to it!"

"Great!" said Zack, excited at the success of their plan. "That should keep them busy for ages. It should be near impossible to find those things in this world."

"Yes, good work, Robobutt," said Eleanor. "You're a smooth operator."

"Smooth operator?" said Robobutt. "What is a smooth operator?"

"Using tears to get the Great White Butt to do what you want!" said Eleanor.

"Using tears?" said Robobutt. "I wasn't 'using' them . . . I was really upset. I want my wedding to be special."

"Of course," said Zack, shooting a look of concern at Eleanor. "Of course! What butt wouldn't?"

"Thank you, Zack," said Robobutt. "I only wish my creator, Ned Smelly, was alive to give me away. He was like a father to me." Robobutt started to cry again.

"Yes," said Zack, worried at how seriously Robobutt seemed to be taking the wedding. "I'm sure Ned would have liked that."

CHAPTER SEVENTY-ONE

Preparations

Zack looked into the sky.

The arseteroid was close now.

Very close.

He clenched his fists.

The future of the world depended on the next two hours.

This was it.

This was what all the butt-kicking, butt-smacking, butt-pinching, butt-forking, butt-flicking, and butt-fighting — real and simulated — had been leading up to.

The final conflict.

It had been a long and smelly road.

Across the Great Windy Desert. Through the Brown Forest. Over the Sea of Butts. Into the heart of a buttcano. Caught in a simulated crapalanche. Trapped inside an underground maggotorium. Sucked into a brown hole. Lost on Uranus. Buried under a giant brown blob.

But the long and smelly road was almost at an end.

Zack sucked in a deep breath as he summoned up the courage, the energy, and the resolve for the battle that would determine the very course of buttolution.

Despite the Blind Butt-feeler's predictions that Zack would be the savior of free men everywhere, Zack had seen and experienced too much to think that success was guaranteed. The Great White Butt was a powerful foe. And most of the cards were stacked in the Great White Butt's favor.

Zack was certain, however, that Robobutt's wedding demands would prove impossible to fulfill, thus buying them the time they needed to launch the nuclear wart-head, immobilize the Great White Butt, and ensure that the giant arseteroid would put an end to both him and his deranged dream of world domination.

This was, after all, a world in which wedding dresses hadn't yet been invented. A world in which flowers were a relatively new — and therefore scarce — buttolutionary product.

And, surely, the chance that "sweet" music could exist in such a world was remote.

But Zack was wrong.

Wrong on all three counts.

CHAPTER SEVENTY-TWO

AWOL

Within an hour the three Great White Butts returned bearing their precious gifts.

The first butt to approach the Great White Butt bowed and scraped the ground.

"I bring a most beautiful dress for your bride," it said as it kneeled and held out the white paper-thin bark of a primitive cocobutt-tree.

Robobutt gasped with pleasure at the sight of it. "It's beautiful," she said, wrapping it around herself like a sarong.

She turned slowly from side to side. "Does my butt — I mean — do *I* look too big in this?" she said to the Great White Butt.

"No. It's perfect," said the Great White Butt. "You look even more beautiful than before."

"You're sure I don't look fat? said Robobutt. "I wish I had time to lose just a few pounds."

"Robobutt seems to be really getting into this 'wedding' thing," said Eleanor quietly to Zack.

"I'm hoping it's just an act," said Zack.

"Me too," said Eleanor, biting her lip.

"It *is* a beautiful dress," said Eleanor's butt.

The second Great White Butt stepped forward with a very impressive bouquet of ferns and grasses that, while not technically flowers, were still very pretty.

They heard Robobutt gasp again, and she brought the plants up to her face as if to smell them.

"Olfactory report indicates molecular breakdown very pleasant. . . ." said Robobutt.

"What's that, my dear?" said the Great White Butt.

"Robobutt!" whispered Zack. "Stop doing Robospeak."

"Sorry," said Robobutt. "It's just that they're *so* beautiful!"

Again Zack and Eleanor traded worried glances. What was happening to Robobutt? She was the onboard computer of a butt-fighting machine, programmed for functionality and practicality. She wasn't set up to appreciate beauty or fashion. What would have been the point? But here she was, apparently breathless with excitement about wedding dresses and flowers. . . . Zack frowned.

Something wasn't quite right.

But there wasn't time to fix it now.

The third butt stepped up.

"Your Great Whiteness," it said. "I present to you the finest wind ensemble in the land. The incomparable, the one and only, Great White Butt Quartet."

Four Great White Butts stepped forward and started making the most unpleasant music that Zack had ever heard.

"That is *so* bad," said Zack.

"Just be grateful that we're in here," said Eleanor. "It probably smells even worse than it sounds."

"I think it rocks," said Zack's butt.

"Yeah," said Eleanor's butt, who was now recovered enough to sway slowly from side to side and tap her foot. "It's got a good beat and you can dance to it."

"It's beautiful," said Robobutt, beginning to cry again.

"So there you have it," said the Great White Butt. "A gorgeous dress, a bridal bouquet, and fine music — all you deserve — all you desired and more. Now can we get married?"

"No!" said Zack, desperately trying to think of another demand. "Say no!"

There was a long silence.

"Well?" said the Great White Butt.

"You heard Zack, Robobutt," said Eleanor. "Tell him no!"

"Oh *yes*," said Robobutt. "We can get married now. I have everything I need."

"Oh *no*!" said Zack. "She ignored our commands!"

"Can we take manual control?" said Eleanor. "Try the override."

Zack pushed the button frantically. "No response," he said. "Robobutt's gone AWOL!"*

---

*AWOL: Arse without leave.

CHAPTER SEVENTY-THREE

Wedding

Zack and Eleanor watched helplessly as the Great White Butt led Robobutt to stand beside him with her back to the assembled butts.

They watched as two small — and strangely familiar — butts appeared in front of them.

"Isn't that . . ." said Eleanor, trying to remember where she'd seen the butts before. "Isn't that *the Prince*?"

"And Maurice!" said Zack's butt.

"Who are they?" said Eleanor's butt.

"Good question," said Zack. "I'm not sure that they know the answer themselves. One minute they're working for the Great White Butt, the next minute they're working against him. Looks like they've gone back to working with him."

"But why?" said Eleanor.

"Why not?" shrugged Zack. "Everyone else seems to be."

"I'm not working for the Great White Butt," said Zack's butt.

"Me neither," said Eleanor's butt.

Zack's butt shuffled nervously in its direction. "Um," it said, "I guess I owe you an apology."

"It's okay," said Eleanor's butt. "You couldn't have known."

"Yeah," said Zack's butt, "but that doesn't make it . . ."

"Shush," said Zack. "It's starting!"

"Sorry," said the two butts in unison.

As they watched, the Prince cleared his throat and began to speak. "We are gathered here today to join these two butts in holy buttrimony."

"Holy buttrimony," echoed Maurice. "Holy, holy buttrimony . . . holy, holy, holy . . ."

"That's enough, Maurice," said the Prince.

Zack bit his lip.

It was all happening too fast.

"We've got to do something!" said Zack. "At this rate they'll have married and left for their honeymoon before the arseteroid has even entered the Earth's atmosphere."

"We've got to launch the nuclear wart-head," said Eleanor. "Hopefully, it will immobilize the Great White Butt and keep him here until the arseteroid hits. We'll do it when they kiss. It's our only chance."

"You're right," said Zack. "I just hope we can launch it. Without Robobutt's cooperation, it may be difficult. And that's assuming it's even functional."

"I'll get out there and launch the darn thing myself if I have to," said Eleanor, her eyes burning.

"If there is anybody here who knows why these two butts should not be joined in holy buttrimony," said the Prince, "let him speak now or forever hold his peace."

"Or forever hold his peace," said Maurice. "Or forever, and ever, and ever . . ."

"Shut up, Maurice!" said the Prince.

"Sorry," said Maurice.

A hush descended upon the crowd. The Prince waited, but nobody spoke.

"Get on with it," said the Great White Butt impatiently.

"Yes, Your Whiteness," said the Prince. "If there is nobody here who objects, then we may proceed. . . ."

"*I* object!" gurgled a strange and unearthly voice. "This wedding must not go ahead!"

CHAPTER SEVENTY-FOUR

Sprung!

There was a collective intake of breath from the assembled crowd.

Zack and Eleanor both gasped. It was a voice that they knew all too well. It was also a voice that neither of them had expected to hear again. Zack looked over his shoulder at the vacuum cleaner.

It was empty.

All that remained of the Mutant Barf Lord was a glistening trail across the floor, which ended at the entrance to the teleportation tube.

"Oh, no," said Zack quietly. "We're in trouble. BIG trouble. The Mutant Barf Lord must have taken advantage of his liquefied state to escape out of the vacuum cleaner!"

"You're right!" said Eleanor, pointing at the screen. "Look!"

The wedding crowd was in uproar.

"Who — and what — are you?" thundered the Great White Butt, staring down at the Mutant Barf Lord, who was now little more than a lumpy puddle on the ground in front of him.

"Just a humble servant, Your Whiteness," said the Mutant Barf Lord puddle. "One that simply wants — and has always wanted — the best for you."

"On what grounds, puddle of vomit," said the Prince, trying to regain control of the proceedings, "do you object to this wedding taking place?"

"Because," said the Mutant Barf Lord puddle with a dramatic pause, "because the bride is not in fact a butt. She is a robot! She is nothing more than a souped-up butt-mobile!"

There was a collective outpouring of methane from the shocked crowd.

But no butt released more methane than the Great White Butt himself.

"What does the Mutant Barf Lord think he's doing?" said Eleanor.

"Revenge," said Zack. "He must have figured that if he can't have what he wanted, than neither can we."

The Great White Butt, blanched and shell-shocked, turned to his bride. "Tell me it's not true!" he begged her. "Tell me it's not true and I'll have this . . . this . . . ."

"Faithful servant," ventured the Mutant Barf Lord puddle helpfully.

"*Whatever it is*," continued the Great White Butt, "scraped up and thrown into the Crack of Doom! Are you really a robot?"

"Tell him it's not true," Eleanor urged Robobutt in the

desperate hope that Robobutt might have regained control of her higher logic functions. "Run while you still can!"

"But this is my wedding," said Robobutt in a halting, confused voice.

"It will be your funeral if you don't run while you've still got the chance," said Eleanor. "Please!"

The Great White Butt repeated his question. "Are you really a robot?"

"Affirmative," said Robobutt. "The puddle of regurgitated zombie blowfly vomit speaks the truth. I am Robobutt. Fully riveted reinforced steel cheeks. Turbo-assisted jet repulsion units. Nuclear wart-head equipped. Matter transport assisted entry and exit. Inside and outside voice options. Onboard tea- and coffee-making facilities. And I am self-wiping!"

The Great White Butt let out a butt-wrenching howl of pure pain. "No!" he cried. "Tell me it's not true!"

"I cannot deny the truth," said Robobutt. "But this doesn't have to change anything, does it?"

"Of course it does!" thundered the Great White Butt. "It changes *everything*. And somebody's going to pay!"

And saying this, the Great White Butt picked Robobutt up by the legs, held her upside down, and began shaking her violently.

"Uh-oh," said Zack. "Hold on, everybody. This could get a little rough."

But it was too late.

And more than a *little* rough.

Eleanor, Zack, and their butts were shaken around

like beans in a can, bouncing and crashing off the walls, roof, and floor.

It was almost a relief when they hit the emergency exit and it popped open, sending them flying out onto the ground in front of the Great White Butt and right into the middle of the Mutant Barf Lord puddle.

Almost.

CHAPTER SEVENTY-FIVE

Puddle

"Get out of me!" said the Mutant Barf Lord puddle.

Zack, Eleanor, and their butts were only too happy to comply with the puddle's request.

"Gross!" said Eleanor, jumping up and brushing the slimy goop off her clothes.

"Double-gross!" said Zack, shaking his arms and hands clear of the stinking muck. Being giant-brown-blobbified had been bad, but this was much, much worse.

Eleanor shook her head. "You should have left him in that web, Zack," she said. "You should have let the buttantula take care of him. We would all have been better off . . . including the Mutant Barf Lord puddle."

"Yeah," said Zack. "I know that *now* . . . but I didn't know it then. If only I could go back and change things I would, but I guess it's not that easy, is it?"

"No," said Eleanor. "*Nothing* is easy."

But as disgusting as they were, the remains of the

Mutant Barf Lord were the least of their worries at that moment.

The Great White Butt was purple with rage.

They looked up at his huge dark cheeks. "You two!" he roared.

"Four, actually," said Zack's butt, pulling Eleanor's butt out of the puddle.

"Whatever!" said the Great White Butt, shaking. "I should have known that you would have one last desperately futile attempt to stop me from fulfilling my dream, but I never suspected that you would stoop as low as this. All is fair in love and war, but to break my heart in this way is unspeakably cruel."

"Well, you'd know all about unspeakable cruelty," said Eleanor. "You killed my mother."

"And mine," said Eleanor's butt.

"And mine," said Zack.

"And mine," said Zack's butt.

"You've been responsible," said Eleanor, "for the deaths of *everyone* we loved, and you have the nerve to accuse *us* of unspeakable cruelty?"

The Great White Butt chuckled. "Flattery will get you nowhere," he said. "But never forget, it was you and your type who made me what I am!"

"By what twisted logic do you come to that conclusion?" said Eleanor.

"It was a long time ago," said the Great White Butt. "Back when I was just a hatchling. I was barely out of my shell when our nest was attacked by butt-fighters. They wiped out my whole family. They tried to kill me, too, but I outflew them. I took refuge on Uranus, where I was treated as a god by the local butts. I stayed for millions of years. I eventually returned to Earth to rejoin my race, but discovered that all of my kind were dead, wiped out by an arseteroid. I realized I was the last of the Great White Butts. I thought I was destined to spend the rest of my life alone. That is, until I discovered the time-travel possibilities of the brown hole."

Zack gulped.

Eleanor glared at Zack.

"Can you imagine what sort of welcome to the world it is to be shot at by butt-fighters?" continued the Great White Butt. "If I am violent and vengeful, it is all *their* fault. *They* made me what I am!"

"Nobody *made* you anything," said Eleanor. "You made yourself."

"Maybe," said the Great White Butt. "And maybe not. What is certain is that I am now making the way clear for the first, last, and greatest life form on the planet!"

"With my help, of course," said the Mutant Barf Lord puddle.

"*Your* help?" said the Great White Butt. "A puddle of vomit?"

"Not just a puddle of vomit, Your Whiteness!" said the Mutant Barf Lord puddle. "Your faithful servant."

"Faithful servant?" said the Great White Butt. "I've never seen you before."

"Sir," said the Mutant Barf Lord puddle. "For many long years I was known as the Kisser . . . working for the B-team . . . but I was a butt-fighter in name only — a double agent — working at every opportunity to sabotage their plans in order to help you establish the new world order. Let me continue to serve you. Let me be your right-hand man! Please . . ."

The Great White Butt regarded the puddle on the ground skeptically. "You don't even *have* a right hand — *or* a left one. And you don't even resemble a man. You look like you've been eaten by maggots, thrown up by flies, and put together again!"

"I have," said the Mutant Barf Lord puddle, bubbling sadly.

CHAPTER SEVENTY-SIX

Mopped Up

The Mutant Barf Lord puddle's reply took the Great White Butt so much by surprise that he began to laugh. The Prince took his cue and began to laugh as well. Maurice and the other Great White Butts joined in and the entire gathering began emitting great gales of methane-fueled mirth.

Zack blocked his nose and looked at the puddle. Its bubbling had been replaced by steaming.

"What I want to know," said the Mutant Barf Lord puddle, as the laughter subsided, "is what's your excuse?"

"I beg your pardon?" said the Great White Butt. "Excuse for what?"

"Your excuse for being a big pimply loser with half of his left cheek missing who doesn't know who his true friends are!" said the Mutant Barf Lord puddle.

Zack caught his breath sharply. It was not a good idea

to talk like this to the Great White Butt. Even if it *was* true.

"Seize that puddle!" said the Great White Butt. "And throw it into the Crack of Doom!"

"But how do we seize a puddle?" said the Prince.

"Mop it up!" said the Great White Butt, exasperated. "Use the robot's dress!"

"No!" whimpered Robobutt, who was lying on the ground. "Not my dress!"

But the Prince and Maurice were unmoved by Robobutt's pleas. They tore at her dress and began using large handfuls of it to soak up the puddle.

"You're making a big mistake!" said what was left of the Mutant Barf Lord.

"I don't make mistakes," said the Great White Butt.

"Yes, you do," said the Mutant Barf Lord puddle. "You fell in love with a robot, you big fat fool."

The Great White Butt roared with fury. He grabbed the soggy pieces of wedding dress containing the Mutant Barf Lord puddle from the startled Prince and Maurice and threw them into the fiery crevice himself.

A huge balloon of flame and steam erupted from the Crack.

And then silence.

CHAPTER SEVENTY-SEVEN

Squash!

The butt-fighters stared dumbly at each other.

Nobody spoke.

They didn't have to.

They all knew what was coming next.

"Prepare to be squashed," said the Great White Butt, surprising no one. "*Very slowly.*"

"You'll never get away with this!" said Zack.

"Oh really?" said the Great White Butt. "And how do you propose to stop me? You are surrounded by thousands of Great White Butts — obedient to my every command — your devious time-traveling butt-mobile is broken, and you are covered in a substance that even I must admit is rather unpleasant, and that's saying something."

"I don't know," said Zack, who knew the Great White Butt had a point, "but we'll think of something."

"Well, you'd better think fast," said the Great White Butt as he began lowering himself.

Zack and Eleanor looked at each other.

Zack's butt and Eleanor's butt looked at each other.

Zack and Eleanor looked at their butts.

Their butts looked at Zack and Eleanor.

There was nowhere to run.

Nowhere to hide.

Nothing to say.

This was it.

They had lost.

All the pain.

All the suffering.

All the bravery.

All the stench.

All for nothing.

The whole glorious history of butt-fighting had come to a dead end.

Humanity was doomed.

The future belonged to the butts.

Eleanor picked up her butt and kissed it good-bye.

Zack hugged his butt tight, closed his eyes, and prepared to be squashed.

Slowly.

CHAPTER SEVENTY-EIGHT

Love

No!" cried a metallic voice.

Zack opened his eyes.

It was Robobutt.

Somehow she had pulled her battered shell and body parts together for one last stand. "Don't do it," she said. "They're not worth it!"

"Thanks a lot!" said Zack.

"I'm sorry," said Robobutt. "But I must follow my heart!"

"But you're a robot," said the Great White Butt.

"Robots have feelings too," said Robobutt. "And my feelings are clear. I love you!"

The Great White Butt flushed pink as it absorbed what Robobutt had said.

Then it flushed red.

Then it flushed a deep shade of crimson.

Its knees buckled.

Its flesh quivered.

"Are you all right, Your Whiteness?" asked the Prince.

"No," said the Great White Butt. "I am not all right. In my life I have experienced much — I have been kicked, smacked, pinched, forked, flicked, shot at, burned, feared, loathed, and universally hated — but I have never experienced this. I have never experienced *love.*"

Robobutt held out her arms.

Zack watched the Great White Butt visibly soften as millions of years of toughness and stinkiness and hatred melted away. He took a few faltering steps toward Robobutt, but old habits clearly died hard. "I am coming," he said to Robobutt, "but first let me sit on them! Make them pay for how I've suffered."

"No," said Robobutt. "Just hold me."

"First I'll squash them, and then I'll hold you," said the Great White Butt.

"No," said Robobutt. "I've got a better idea. How about first you hold me and then we'll squash them together!"

"You traitor!" said Eleanor. "I'm glad Ned Smelly's not alive to see this."

"Great butts think alike!" exclaimed the Great White Butt, stepping into Robobutt's embrace. "I can see we're going to have a long and happy life together!"

"Happy?" said Robobutt. "What is 'happy'?"

"This, you big dummy!" said the Great White Butt, reaching out to Robobutt.

"Oh, darling," said Robobutt as the two gigantic butts

embraced over the top of the disbelieving — and completely grossed-out — butt-fighters.

"Yuck!" said Zack's butt.

"Now I've seen *everything*," said Eleanor.

But Eleanor had spoken too soon.

Suddenly there was a loud crackling and hissing, and black smoke began to pour from Robobutt's crumpled shell.

"What's the matter?" said the Great White Butt. "What's happening to you?"

"Circuit overload . . ." spluttered Robobutt. "My system was not designed for 'happy.' . . ."

"NO!" cried the Great White Butt. "I lost you once! I couldn't stand to lose you again!"

But there was no response from Robobutt.

She was completely fused, her arms still locked around the Great White Butt.

CHAPTER SEVENTY-NINE

Boom!

As the Great White Butt struggled to escape Robobutt's embrace, there was a new commotion among the Great White Butts.

They were all pointing to the enormous blazing ball of doom hurtling toward them.

"Master!" cried the Prince. "We must leave! The arse-teroid is about to strike! We cannot delay any longer!"

"I can't move!" said the Great White Butt. "Robobutt has me locked in an unbreakable hug!"

"It's too late for you now!" said Zack, with renewed hope. "Too late for you and your demented dream of world buttination!"

But the Great White Butt's only response was to laugh. "You stupid little boy," he chuckled. "You don't get it, do you?"

"I get it all right," said Zack. "You — the most evil

butt in history — are about to be destroyed . . . *once and for all.*"

"That's where you're wrong," said the Great White Butt. "I may be destroyed, but I won't be *destroyed.*"

"Huh?" said Zack.

"Let me put it another way," said the Great White Butt. "You can destroy me, but you can't destroy *me.*"

"Ignore him, Zack," said Eleanor. "He's got methane madness."

"You wish," said the Great White Butt, "but I can assure you that I'm perfectly sane — although I think it's only fair to warn you, I'm going to be a little angry when I return from Uranus and find out what's happened."

"You're not *on* Uranus," said Eleanor.

"Oh yes I am," said the Great White Butt.

"You're on Earth!" said Zack.

"That is true," said the Great White Butt, "but I'm *also* on Uranus. Remember?"

"Oh no . . ." said Zack, as the awful truth began to dawn on him. The reason the Great White Butt hadn't been killed in the original arseteroid collision was because he had been on Uranus at the time. He had only returned to Earth *after* the arseteroid had hit. But the arseteroid hadn't hit yet. And so the younger version of the Great White Butt that Zack had disturbed and chased five hundred and eighty-five million years ago was *still* on Uranus. The Great White Butt was right. They could destroy him now, but it wouldn't mean they had destroyed him forever. The younger Great White Butt would return from Uranus. Buttageddon would still happen.

Eleanor groaned. Zack turned to look at her. She had

her head in her hands. It was obvious she'd realized the same thing.

"We've failed," said Eleanor. "Despite everything we've done, we haven't really changed anything."

"No," said Zack sadly. "There are two Great White Butts. And we can only destroy one."

"I guess I should be thanking you," roared the Great White Butt triumphantly. "After all, with enemies like you, who needs friends?"

"You do!" said Zack's butt.

"Forget it," said Zack. "It's over."

"It's over all right," said Zack's butt. "Over for the Great White Butt. Me and Robobutt already took care of it."

"Took care of what?" said Zack.

"The Great White Butt on Uranus," said Zack's butt. "While you and Eleanor were rescuing Eleanor's butt, and before the Mutant Barf Lord went crazy, Robobutt and I were discussing the problem. . . ."

"You *knew* about the other Great White Butt?" said Zack. "Why didn't you say anything?"

"You were busy," said Zack's butt. "And it was very complicated. Anyway, to cut a long story short, we thought it best if I aimed Robobutt's interplanetary death ray at Uranus and gave it a quick zap. Just to be on the safe side. If Robobutt's calculations are correct, the death ray should be arriving on Uranus right about now, eradicating any form of life — including Great White Butts — on the planet."

The Great White Butt gave a long loud moan of pain.

Zack and Eleanor stared dumbfounded at Zack's butt.

"I didn't know Robobutt had an interplanetary death ray," said Zack.

"There's a lot you don't know," said Zack's butt. "But it doesn't matter. You've got me."

"I may not know much," said Zack, shaking his head in wonder at his resourceful butt, "but I do know one thing. You're the best butt a boy could ever wish for."

Zack's butt reddened at the compliment.

Eleanor's butt looked on admiringly.

"Well done, soldier," said Eleanor quietly. "Well done."

The Great White Butt moaned again — longer and even more loudly than before. The game was up. And he knew it.

"Eat arseteroid, you freak!" shouted Eleanor.

"You'll be eating it with me!" said the Great White Butt. "At least I have that small consolation. You can no more escape than I can!"

"It doesn't matter to us," said Zack, now finally understanding what his gran had meant back in the stinkant cave. "Where would we escape to, anyway? This is where we *need* to be. Right here. Right now. This is what our whole lives have been leading up to. Because of us the human race will be free to evolve without you constantly inciting our butts to rebellion. Because of us, butts will be free to work *with* their bodies instead of against them. There'll be no need for them to grow independent arms and legs and run around pursuing their own selfish interests. . . ."

"I don't know if I like the sound of that," said Zack's butt.

"It doesn't matter what you like or dislike," said Zack. "That's the whole point! Human beings will be completely integrated. No part will be more important than any other. All parts will work together in perfect harmony."

"I *definitely* don't like it," said Zack's butt.

"Me, neither," said Eleanor's butt.

"Don't worry about it," said Eleanor, shielding her eyes against the heat and brightness of the arseteroid, which was now only minutes away from impact. "You won't be around not to like it, anyway. None of us will!"

"So long," said Eleanor's butt. "It was good knowing you."

"You too," said Eleanor hugging her butt tight. "And you, Zack," she added, touching his arm. "And your stupid butt. I'm going to miss you both."

"I'll miss you both, too," said Zack's butt, his voice cracking with emotion.

"Good-bye, Eleanor," said Zack. "And thanks. Thanks for everything."

"And?" said Zack's butt.

"And what?" said Zack.

"Is there somebody else you want to thank?" said his butt.

"Ummm," said Zack, ". . . oh yes! Of course." He turned to Eleanor's butt. "Thank you!"

"Don't mention it," said Eleanor's butt.

"I hate you, Zack," said Zack's butt.

"Oh well," said Zack, reaching out and embracing his butt. "Can't win them all, I guess."

His butt softened instantly and hugged him back.

The heat and light from the arseteroid were intense.

Suddenly Zack and his butt were drenched by an evil-smelling liquid.

"Errggghh, gross!" said Zack, wiping his face with his sleeve. "What's that?"

"I don't know," said his butt, looking up, "but I think it's a tear. The Great White Butt is crying!"

Zack, Eleanor, and Eleanor's butt looked up as well to see the Great White Butt as they'd never seen him before.

Not "great" at all.

Instead they saw a sad, defeated butt standing at a crooked angle with sagging cheeks. Locked in the deadly embrace of a broken robot. Weeping.

"All I have worked for," he sobbed. "All I have lived for. All I have dreamed of. All for nothing. I've lost every-thing, including the only butt that I've ever loved. All gone. All past. All finished."

"See you in Butthalla!" shouted Zack as the fatal arse-teroid completed the last few feet of its history-making voyage and slammed into Earth.

CHAPTER EIGHTY

Butthalla?

Zack blinked.
    And blinked again.
    But he couldn't see anything.
He wondered if he was dead.
Then he heard a screech.
Oh no, he thought.
It's not over.
What was it now?
A deadly tyrannosore-arse on the prowl?
A tricerabutt getting ready to charge?
A pouncing poopasaur?
A buttodactyl swooping in to carry him away to its nest in the mountains?
But more important than "what" was "why."
Why was he hearing anything at all?
He was supposed to be dead.
He'd just been hit by an arseteroid the size of a major

city with three thousand trillion megatons of destructive force. Enough force to completely wipe out ninety-five percent of life and utterly change the course of history on Earth forever. Zack was a tough butt-fighter — that was for sure — but no butt-fighter was tough enough to survive an impact like that.

So, he figured, he *must* be dead.

And if he was dead, was he in Butthalla?

Zack heard the tyrannosore-arse screech again and frowned.

If this *was* Butthalla, then what was a tyrannosore-arse doing here?

He blinked again and, discovering with relief that he was now able to see, looked around him.

It sure didn't *look* like Butthalla.

Butthalla was supposed to be a glorious place where great butt-fighting warriors gathered to celebrate their heroic butt-fighting days.

But what Zack saw was just a cobweb-covered corrugated-iron roof only a few yards away from his face.

It wasn't exactly what he'd expected Butthalla to look like.

Somehow he'd expected the decor to be a little more upscale.

A little more befitting honored butt-fighters.

Pressed gold ceilings, for instance.

Not cobwebs.

A large black spider crawled lazily across the roof toward a small fly struggling on its web.

Zack shivered as he watched the fly. He knew all too

well how that felt. He reached up and pulled the fly free from the web.

Sitting up, he realized he was a long way off the ground.

He was sitting on top of an enormous stack of hay bales.

There was a gap, and on the other side of the gap there was another large stack of hay bales.

Smoke was wafting into the building from somewhere outside.

Old rusty pieces of machinery and contraptions were hanging from the walls.

He heard the screech again.

But now it sounded less like a tyrannosore-arse and much more like a rooster.

Zack blinked again.

Nope.

He wasn't in Butthalla.

He was sure of that much.

And he wasn't on prehistoric Earth.

As far as he could tell, the only immediate danger he faced was falling off the hay bale and being attacked by a rooster.

But what about Eleanor?

Where was she?

CHAPTER EIGHTY-ONE

Barnhalla

Eleanor?" called Zack.

There was no response.

"Eleanor?" he called even louder.

"Zack?" said a voice from the top of the other hay bale stack. "Where are we? Are we dead?"

"I'm not too sure," said Zack. "But I don't think so. We seem to be in a barn."

Zack watched as Eleanor sat up and rubbed her eyes. She coughed.

"How did we get here?" she said, peering over the edge of the stack and toward the open door, where there seemed to be some sort of bonfire burning. "And where are our butts?"

"I don't know," said Zack. "Apparently this is what happens when you're hit by a gigantic arseteroid from outer space. You wake up in a barn with no butt."

"I would have preferred Butthalla," said Eleanor.

"Me too," said Zack. "But who's complaining? At least we're alive."

"Or we're dreaming," said Eleanor.

"Even if we're dreaming, we're still alive!" said Zack.

"Not necessarily," said Eleanor. "We could be dead and just dreaming that we're dreaming that we're still alive."

"But that's stupid," said Zack, raising his voice. "If we were dead, how could we . . ."

"You'll be dead if you don't get out of my barn right now!" yelled a figure standing in the doorway. "How many times do I have to tell you kids that it's not safe to play up there? Your mothers will kill me if they find out!"

Zack and Eleanor both stared at the figure in the doorway. It was bright, and their eyes were having trouble adjusting to the light, but as they did they saw, to their surprise, that it was Ned Smelly.

"Ned?" said Zack, wondering why he was dressed in a pair of farmer's overalls instead of his traditional buttfighting armor.

"Ned?!" said Ned, walking over to the middle of the bales as Eleanor and Zack climbed down. "Who's Ned?"

Zack looked at Ned and grinned.

"Why, you of course!" he said. "You're Ned. Ned Smelly!"

"All right, that does it!" said Ned, his face turning crimson with anger. "I've had enough of you two! Get out of here and don't even think about coming back again until you've learned some respect!"

Zack and Eleanor stood there, too surprised by Ned's outburst to move.

"Well?" he said. "What are you waiting for? Git!"

He waved his pitchfork and moved toward them threateningly, but Zack and Eleanor didn't need any more encouragement to leave.

They ran.

EIGHTY-TWO

Ed

Zack and Eleanor ran out of the barn, past a smoking bonfire, and down a long dirt driveway.

They didn't stop running until they came to a gate. They clambered over it and stood on the other side trying to catch their breath.

"What was all that about?" said Eleanor. "Why do you think Ned was upset?"

Zack was holding on to a mailbox as he panted, and noticed a small painted sign hanging from the bottom.

"I don't know," said Zack. "But I think it might have something to do with the fact that his name is not Ned Smelly."

"Huh?" said Eleanor, standing up with her hands on her hips, looking back up the driveway in case Ned Smelly was coming after them. "Of course that was Ned. Wasn't it?"

"Not according to this sign here," said Zack.

Eleanor bent down and studied it carefully. "Ed . . . Kelly . . ." she said, reading aloud. "Ed Kelly?"

"Ed Kelly," said Zack nodding.

After she had stared at it for a long while, Eleanor rose up slowly. "Zack," she said. "Something's happened. Something big."

"I know," said Zack, nodding. "But *what* exactly . . . and why are you staring at my butt?"

"Because it's where it's *supposed* to be, Zack," said Eleanor, patting her rear. "And so is mine!"

Zack reached around and patted his butt. Of all the strange things that had happened in the last few minutes, this was the strangest of all. His butt had been running around by itself for so long that he could hardly remember when it was last attached.

"Are you okay?" he said.

But there was no reply.

"Hey!" said Zack. "Say something!"

He knew it was a dangerous command to give to his butt, but it remained silent.

"You're right," said Zack to Eleanor. "Something's horribly wrong. I'm worried."

"I didn't say something's horribly wrong," said Eleanor. "In fact, I think it might be the other way around. I think that — for a change — something might have gone horribly *right*."

"Eleanor," said Zack, "you must still be suffering methane madness — or at least you've inhaled too much of that bonfire smoke! Ned Smelly thinks he's somebody called *Ed Kelly*? And my butt isn't running around being cheeky? How can you call that 'horribly right'?"

"Because *it's exactly what we wanted*, you idiot!" said Eleanor.

"But I thought 'Ned Smelly' was a good name," said Zack.

"Not that," said Eleanor, "though that's part of it. No, what I mean is that we've succeeded in creating a future where butts are *just* butts. The Great White Butt has been destroyed and the world has evolved exactly as it would have if he hadn't been encouraging butts to rebel against their owners for so many thousands of years!"

CHAPTER EIGHTY-THREE

Butt-Free!

Zack thought carefully.

Perhaps Eleanor was right.

If she was, it would certainly help to make sense of the Blind Butt-feeler's predictions: "Zack Freeman . . . savior of free men everywhere . . . past, present, *and future*. . . ." Here they were in the future and men were now, apparently, free. But it still didn't make sense, thought Zack.

"You're forgetting one thing, Eleanor," said Zack, frowning. "We were directly underneath that arseteroid. Whether or not we succeeded, we shouldn't *be* in the future. We shouldn't be anything apart from a couple of fossils at the center of the Earth."

"You're wrong, Zack," said Eleanor. "We weren't *directly* underneath the arseteroid. Don't you remember? We were underneath the Great White Butt and Robobutt."

"You think we were protected from the force of that arseteroid by a couple of butts?" said Zack.

"Not just ANY couple of butts," said Eleanor. "The combination of the Great White Butt's blubber and the fully riveted reinforced steel cheeks of Robobutt may have been enough to shield us from the worst of it."

"But even if that's true, how did we end up here?" said Zack. "Why aren't we just sitting around on the smoking shell of a dying Earth? The impact of that thing would have been incredible, inconceivably violent — nobody could have survived it. Not even us!"

"Nobody's supposed to have been able to travel through a brown hole and survive, either," said Eleanor. "But *we* did."

"Maybe we were just lucky," said Zack.

"Maybe," said Eleanor. "And then again, maybe not. Brown holes are the result of an extraordinary amount of force. It's possible that at the moment of the arseteroid's impact the force was *so* great that a temporary brown hole was created. A hole through time and space lasting only a mere instant — but long enough to suck us back to the future and spit us out in the present."

"But," said Zack, "that means the Great White Butt might have survived the blast and been sucked back here as well!"

"No," said Eleanor, shaking her head. "Definitely not."

"How can you be so sure?" said Zack.

"Because if he had been, our butts wouldn't be so much a part of us. They'd be running free. No, he — and Robobutt — were destroyed in the blast. We were transported back. Evolution has been able to develop the rest of the world without the interference of the Great White Butt. Give or take a few minor details, of course."

Zack pondered Eleanor's words.

"So we're the only survivors. . . ." he said. "Just us and Ned . . . I mean, *Ed* . . ."

"Maybe," said Eleanor, her eyes widening. "And maybe not. Did you hear what Ned — I mean *Ed* — said? He said, 'Your mothers will kill me.' *Mothers*, Zack. He said *mothers*!"

CHAPTER EIGHTY-FOUR

Homecoming

Zack could see exactly where Eleanor was going.

"Come on, Zack," she said excitedly. "Let's go home!"

"Wait!" said Zack, grabbing her shoulders and making her face him.

"What?" said Eleanor, impatiently, "Don't you see, Zack? In a Great White Butt–free world there was no Great White Butt to kill my mother . . . my mother is still *alive!* I've got to see her!"

"Be careful, Eleanor," said Zack. "If everything you've said is right then, yes, she *could* be alive. But she might not be the same as you remember her."

"I hardly remember her at all, anyway," said Eleanor. "I was only four when she died."

"I'm just saying don't get your hopes up too high," said Zack. "That's all."

Eleanor nodded. "All right, Mr. Gloomy," she said. "Can we go now?"

"Wait," said Zack. "One more thing. We'd better not tell anybody about what we've been through. If you're right, and there's no such thing as runaway butts and butt-fighters in this world, then they'll think we've gone insane."

But Eleanor was already running.

Zack took off after her.

CHAPTER EIGHTY-FIVE

Marbleton

Zack and Eleanor ran all the way from Ed Kelly's farm into Mabeltown. But as they passed the Mabeltown sign they were in for another surprise. It didn't say Mabeltown. It said: MARBLETON.

Even so, the change didn't faze them too much. Not after their run-in with Ed Kelly. They were starting to get the hang of the new world. Everything was the same, just slightly different. Or was it that everything was different, but just slightly the same?

Neither Zack nor Eleanor particularly cared as they ran through the streets of Marbleton, which Zack was relieved to see was exactly the same as Mabeltown except that it bore no evidence of the devastating butt attacks that he had witnessed the last few times he was there.

There weren't even any skidmarks on the road, except for those left by cars.

"Not like that!" yelled a familiar voice, as they hurried

past the local soccer field. A large, brawny soccer coach wearing a shirt with black-and-white stripes and cut-off sleeves was showing a group of kids how to kick a soccer ball.

Zack smiled and pointed him out to Eleanor.

"Look," he said. "It's the Kicker!"

Eleanor nodded and smiled, too, as the Kicker dropped the ball onto his cleat and kicked it clear out of the field.

"*That's* how you kick a ball," he yelled at the terrified children.

"Same old Kicker!" said Zack.

"Yeah," said Eleanor. "Some things never change."

They turned the corner onto the main street. As they passed the local bakery, they heard a series of sharp cracks. The sign on the window read S. MCKERR'S BAKERY. They could see a large woman brutally kneading and smacking a lump of dough into submission.

"The Smacker!" said Zack. "I've really missed that sound!"

Suddenly Eleanor clutched Zack's arm. "Zack!" she said, pointing at a shop across the road. "Look! Captain Sterne's Fishing Supplies!"

Zack's eyes grew wide. The window was full of fishing rods, tackle boxes, nets, rubber boots, full-body wetsuits, and a range of lethal-looking spear guns. One of the larger spear guns looked just like the butt-harpoon that Zack had used to shoot the Great White Butt.

"Do you think . . ." he said.

"Yes!" said Eleanor, walking even faster.

"Look over there!" said Zack, as they approached a

small used-car lot that was surrounded by strings of colored flags.

A well-dressed man with a mustache and slicked-back hair was standing outside watching them as they passed. Zack stared at him. It was the Kisser!

"Good afternoon," he called. "Either of you interested in a car? I have some great bargains . . . how about a fun-mobile?" he said, pointing to a little dune buggy.

"Cool," said Zack. "But I'm not old enough to drive."

"Pity," said the used-car salesman, looking at Zack with a twinkle in his eye. "I think it would really suit you. Come back when you're old enough. I'll give you a very special deal. Trust me!"

"Thanks," said Zack, winking at Eleanor. The Kisser sure looked a lot better than when they'd last seen him, but he was still up to his old tricks.

"See?" said Eleanor, when they were well past. "The details might be different, but the people underneath are still the same."

"Yeah," said Zack, with butterflies in his stomach.

They were approaching his grandmother's street.

"I hope you're right. . . ." he said. "I really do."

CHAPTER EIGHTY-SIX

Alive!

As they walked down his gran's street, Zack was startled by a cat jumping out from behind a tree. It rolled on its back in playful recognition of him.

"Mittens!" said Zack, overjoyed to see her alive again. He kneeled down and patted her head. As he did so, he imagined that he felt his butt twitch. His butt and Mittens had never gotten along very well.

"It's not Mittens, Zack!" said his gran's voice. "It's *Muffin.*"

Zack looked over the fence into his gran's frontyard. There, bent over a bed of pink snapdragons, was his gran. She was pulling weeds out of the ground with the strong fingers that had made her famous as the Pincher.

"Leave the boy alone, Mabel," said an old man who

was balanced on top of a small stepladder, washing the front window of the house. He was wiping the glass dry with a large handful of newspaper. "Mittens, Muffin . . . what's the difference? It's all the same to a cat. How are you, Zack?"

Zack was too stunned to speak.

It was one thing to see your grandmother who died sixty-five million years ago alive again, but to discover that your long-dead grandfather who you'd never even met was still very much alive was another thing entirely. It was Percy. *Percy Freeman. The Wiper!*

"Hi, Grandpa," said Zack, his voice sounding very far away to him, as if speaking in a dream. "It's a great honor to meet you." His grandpa gave Zack a strange look. "I mean, *see* you," said Zack, flustered as he realized his mistake. "It's good to *see* you again!"

"It's good to see you again, too, Zack," said his grandpa, chuckling. "Even though you've only been gone since this morning."

Zack looked at Eleanor and frowned. "I have?" said Zack.

"Are you feeling all right, Zack?" said Gran.

"Yes," said Zack quickly. "I'm fine. Are . . . are . . . Mom and Dad home?"

"They're over at Eleanor's house," said his gran.

Zack turned to Eleanor. "They're alive!" he said.

"Of course they're alive, you silly boy!" said Gran, peering closely at Zack. "I think you must have been out in the sun too long today."

"No," said Zack. "I just forgot."

Gran shook her head and laughed. "You forgot your parents were alive?" she said. "You'd forget your own head if it wasn't screwed on!"

"It's not Zack's head that's the problem," said Eleanor. "It's his butt."

"Language, young lady!" said Gran.

"Sorry," said Eleanor.

Grandpa winked at Zack and Eleanor, trying to suppress a grin.

Zack smiled. The details were different, but the important things hadn't changed. She was still the same old Gran.

"Anyway," she said, "you two had better go along to Eleanor's house. You're having dinner there tonight — or had you forgotten that as well? They'll be wondering where you are."

Even as she spoke, Eleanor and Zack heard a voice calling to them from across the street. They looked and saw two men sitting on the veranda at the front of the house.

"Eleanor! Zack!" boomed a deep voice. "Dinner's almost ready!"

"That's my dad," said Eleanor, her eyes shining.

"You'd better go," said Zack's grandpa.

"See you later," said Zack, as he ran to catch up with Eleanor, who was already halfway across the street. "Have a good night."

"You too," called Gran. "And don't forget to wash your hands!"

CHAPTER EIGHTY-SEVEN

Stories

Zack stared as he approached the house. His father was sitting next to Silas Sterne.

"They *are* alive!" said Zack as he fell into step with Eleanor.

"Yes," said Eleanor. "But what about our mothers? Where are they?"

"Probably inside," said Zack.

"I hope you're right," said Eleanor, biting her lip.

The two butt-fighters — or to be more accurate, ex-butt-fighters — walked up the front steps. Smoke filled the air.

". . . but you know, Jim," said Eleanor's father, a red glow coming from the end of his pipe. "I don't think I'll ever forget the call of the Great White Whale. It will haunt me to the end of my days."

"In a strange way, I know exactly what you mean, Captain," said Jim Freeman. "Once in the middle of a symphony my bassoon made a noise very similar to that of a whale. An interesting sound, to be sure, but definitely not appropriate for that passage. The conductor never forgave me. I think that sound will haunt me to the end of my days as well."

"So you really *do* play a wind instrument," said Zack, shaking his head in wonder. "In an orchestra!"

"Of course I do!" said Jim. "You know that!"

"About time you two showed up," said Captain Sterne, turning his attention to Eleanor. He opened his arms wide. "You were supposed to be home an hour ago!"

"Sorry, Dad," said Eleanor, embracing her father.

"You two haven't been playing in Ed Kelly's barn again, have you?" said Captain Sterne, pulling a bit of straw out of Eleanor's hair.

"No," said Eleanor, straining to see into the kitchen through the screen door. "Is Mom inside?"

"Yes," said the Captain. "She's with Judi."

"I'll just go and tell her that we're okay," Eleanor said, rushing inside.

The screen door banged shut behind her.

"Always on a mission, that girl," said Captain Sterne.

"Just like her father," chuckled Jim.

The Captain fixed Zack with a glittering eye as he packed a new pipe. "I was just telling your dad about the great white whale."

"The Great White Whale?!" said Zack.

"Yes," said the Captain, staring into the distance and repeating the words slowly. "The Great White Whale. . . ."

Zack nodded distractedly. He was more interested in the sight of Eleanor hugging her mother. And the sight of his own mother standing next to them.

"Have you ever read *Moby Dick,* Zack?" said Silas.

"No," said Zack, desperately trying to hear what Eleanor was saying to her mother above the Captain's ramblings.

"I had to rescue Zack from a drain . . . and then we got lost in the desert . . . Brown Forest . . . Sea of Butts . . . buttcano . . . zombie butts . . . maggots . . . brown hole . . . Uranus . . . dawn of life . . . buttosaurs . . . buttantula . . . buttodactyl nest . . . Stink Kong . . . Crack of Doom . . . Great White Butt . . ."

Zack heard Eleanor's mother laugh. "What an imagination you have!" she said.

"We *didn't* imagine it!" said Eleanor. "It really happened!"

Eleanor's mother, a kind woman with soft eyes, put her arm around Eleanor's shoulder and walked her to the door. "You're not boring Zack with another one of your 'true' stories, are you?" she said to her husband. "It's easy to see where you get it from, Eleanor, with a father like that!"

"But, Mom!" said Eleanor. "It's not a *story*! I'm telling the truth!"

Zack's mother looked at Zack. "Eleanor's been telling us that you've had a very big adventure this afternoon," she said, smiling.

"Tell them it's true, Zack," pleaded Eleanor. "They think I'm making it up!"

"Don't believe a word of it," said Zack firmly, frowning at Eleanor. "It was just a game."

Eleanor glared back at him.

"I'm glad I can count on at least one of you to tell the truth!" said Eleanor's mother, shaking her head. "Now go and get washed up for dinner."

CHAPTER EIGHTY-EIGHT

Beginnings

In the bathroom Zack and Eleanor washed their hands.

"We can't tell *anybody* about what happened and what we've been through," said Zack, toweling his hands dry. "They'll never understand. They *can't* understand."

"I know," said Eleanor. "Sorry, I forgot. Seeing Mom again after all these years . . . I didn't know what I was saying. I still can't really believe it."

"Yeah," said Zack, nodding. "It's weird. It doesn't seem real. And yet it is. We did it, Eleanor. *We saved the world!*"

Eleanor turned the tap off. "Do you think so?" she said. "Really? You don't think there's even a slight chance that the Great White Butt survived? Remember what the Mutant Barf Lord said? 'The Great White Butt is a freak.' How do we know that he didn't survive the blast . . . that he's not out there somewhere . . . plotting . . . planning . . . preparing another Buttageddon?"

Zack put his hands on Eleanor's shoulders. "Because we're here now," said Zack. "That's how. You said it yourself!"

Eleanor nodded slowly. "Yes," she said. "But . . ."

"No buts," said Zack. "Although it only feels like an hour ago to us, the arseteroid blast happened sixty-five million years ago. If the Great White Butt had survived, he would have tried something by now, don't you think? But there's no evidence of it. We're living in a world where there are no such things as butt-fighting or butt-fighters. Except for us, of course. We'll always be butt-fighters. And it is up to us to guard the Earth against the remote possibility of butt attacks in the future. We've both taken the butt-fighter's oath, after all. But we're the only ones who can ever possibly know what really happened and what we achieved."

"Only us," said Eleanor, "and our butts."

"No." said Zack. "Not even our butts, remember? They're not independent operators anymore."

As Zack said this, he patted his butt — and froze.

"What's the matter?" said Eleanor.

"It's gone!" said Zack. "My butt's gone!"

Eleanor patted the back of her pants and gasped. "So has mine!" she said. "Oh no! Not again! It's *not* over, is it?"

The two ex-butt fighters stared at each other for a long, horrifying moment.

Then Zack grinned.

"Why are you smiling, Zack?" said Eleanor. "This isn't funny!"

"Look!" said Zack, pointing over Eleanor's shoulder.

Eleanor turned. Then she grinned too.

Their two butts were standing on the window ledge, hand in hand, gazing at the sunset.

Eleanor and Zack stood and watched their butts watching the sunset.

It was a beautiful scene.

Well, beautiful until Zack's butt did a long, loud fart.

Eleanor's butt reddened, turned to Zack's butt, and then, to both Zack and Eleanor's surprise, replied in kind.

The two butts nudged closer to each other as their gases mingled and combined into a perfect love heart above them.

Zack, his eyes watering, looked at Eleanor and smiled. "No," he said. "I don't think it's over yet. Not by a long shot. In fact, I think it's only just begun."

Glossary

Accident
Another word for *fate*.

Anti-giant-brown-blob spray
Provides personal protection against *giant-brown-blobbification*.

Arseteroid
Irregularly shaped butt that orbits the Sun. They range in size from a 1,000-mile diameter down to dust particles. Occasionally they slam into the Earth. Avoid. See *giant arseteroid*.

Atomic butt-blasting bullets
Butt-gun bullets with atomic butt-blasting power.

Atomic power punch
A powerful punch delivered to a butt or butts. May be delivered with one fist or two. See *double-handed atomic power punch*.

AWOL
Arse without leave.

B-force
Unit of force based on the amount of energy it takes one butt to kick another butt one yard.

Blind Butt-feeler, The
A person with the power to "read" butts and reveal amazing — and frequently mystifying — information about the past, present, and future.

Blob-boy
Insulting term used to describe young *butt-fighters* who have been found fossilized inside fossilized *giant brown blobs*.

Book of Buttageddon, The
Ancient text that contains a prophecy of *Buttageddon*: "And enormous butts will conquer the world and complete and utter devarsetation will follow. *Giant brown blobs* will rain down upon the Earth for forty days and forty nights. An evil stench will cover the land. And the reign of the *Great White Butts* will begin. Butts will rule the world again as they did in their glorious prehistoric past."

BPS
Short for butt positioning system. A means of determining geographical location by means of one's butt.

Brown Forest, The
Formerly known as the Black Forest, this once healthy and thriving forest is now dead and brown and full of *stinkbogs* due to the presence of the Great Unwiped Butt, *Stenchgantor*. Avoid.

Brown holes
Very similar to black holes except brown. They are formed when vast interstellar butts run out of gas and collapse under the power of their own repulsive stench, which reverses itself and endows the newly formed brown holes with the power to suck anything and everything into themselves. Nobody knows what happens to matter sucked into a brown hole, but there is a strong possibility that the forces inside a brown hole are strong enough to form wormholes in the fabric of the *univarse* — wormholes powerful enough to allow vast interstellar distances to be traveled in the blink of an eye or even, perhaps, to permit time travel.

Brown Lake, The
Waste usually found at the bottom chamber of a *buttcano*. Avoid.

B-team, The
A crack butt-fighting unit made up of *the Kicker, the Kisser,* and *the Smacker*.

Butt
The two fleshy mounds above the legs and below the hollow of the back. Detachable, with a will of their own. May emit gas. See *fart*.

Buttageddon
Destruction of the world by butts. Avoid. See *Book of Buttageddon, The*.

Buttageddonized
To be destroyed by *Buttageddon*.

Buttantula
A large prehistoric butt with hairy cheeks, big sharp fangs, and eight legs. Likes to build webs across ravines and catch *buttodactyls* and unwary *butt-fighters*. Avoid.

Butt attack
Physical, either by ground, sea, or air by one — or more — butts. Avoid.

Buttbliteration
Result of particularly devastating *butt attack*. Avoid.

Buttcam
Tiny camera fitted on a butt. Can provide 180 degrees of vision. May be linked to other buttcams around the Earth via satellite to provide a comprehensive butt's-eye view of the world.

Buttcano
An extinct volcano colonized by butts and filled with lethal amounts of methane. Avoid.

Butt creeper
Rampant creeping plant notable for noxious-smelling flowers. Avoid.

Butt-fighter
Any individual engaged in butt-resistance, in either a paid or voluntary capacity.

Butt-fighters' Army pocket knife
A pocket knife with many additional items that fold into its handle, e.g., butt-screw, butt-file, and butt-opener.

Butt-fighter's certificate
The minimum qualification required to become a professional *butt-fighter*. Involves a basic grounding in all aspects of attack, defense, and hygiene.

Butt-fighting recruits
Promising young members of the *Junior Butt-fighters' League* who have been selected for a place at *Silas Sterne's Butt-fighting Academy.*

Butt-fighting simulator
Virtual-reality machine invented by *Silas Sterne* to simulate a wide range of butt-fighting environments and challenges, used for training rookie *butt-fighters.* The simulator is so powerful that the users forget they are in

a simulated environment and actually believe that they are fighting butts.

Butt-gun
All-purpose anti-butt weapon. Fires a wide variety of ammunition, including thumbtacks, staples, and rusty nails.

Butthalla
A glorious place in the sky where great *butt-fighters* and *butt-hunters* go after they die.

Butt Hunter
A butt-warrior who has given up regular butt-fighting in order to concentrate his or her energies on hunting big-game butts. This occupation is so fraught with danger that only a few of the bravest, most talented, and smartest butt hunters survive.

Butt-mobile
Multipurpose all-terrain butt-fighting vehicle. May have time travel capability.

Buttodactyl
Extinct flying butts of the Jurassic and Cretaceous periods. Has membranous, leathery cheek-wings and a rudimentary but razor-sharp beak. Avoid.

Buttolution
Theory that butts were the first form of life on Earth and

that all subsequent life forms developed from them. See *Sir Roger Francis Rectum*.

Buttosaur
Extinct butts that ruled the Earth for hundreds of millions of years until the impact of a *giant arseteroid* rendered the Earth unsuitable for the continuation of the species. See *buttantula, buttodactyl, Great White Buttosaur, poopasaur, Stink Kong, tricerabutt, tyrannosore-arse*.

Buttquake
Just like an earthquake, only wobblier. And smellier. Avoid.

Butt-to-butt resuscitation
A method that butts use to revive each other.

Captain Sterne's Fishing Supplies
A comprehensive one-stop fishing supplies shop in *Marbleton*. Fresh bait every day.

Catastrophic time travel error
Going back into the past and altering something that changes things in such a way that it decreases or eliminates the chance of you being born in the future. Or destroys the world. Avoid.

Cocobutts
The fruit of *cocobutt-trees*. These are similar to coconuts except the shells are soft and consist of two main

chambers rather than one. Cocobutts are edible, but taste like burnt toast.

Cocobutt-trees
Very similar to coconut trees, with a tuft of branches sticking out of a long slender trunk. *Cocobutts*, which look like butts, grow in bunches on the branches.

Crack of Doom, The
Formed by a dramatic fissure in the earth. Breeding ground of the *Great White Buttosaurs*.

Crapalanche
Just like an avalanche except crappier. And browner. And smellier. Avoid.

Destiny
Another word for *fate*.

Dirty double-crossing stinkant-butt-kissing loser with no friends
A very nasty thing to say to somebody . . . even if they *are* a dirty double-crossing stinkant-butt-kissing loser with no friends.

Double-handed atomic power punch
A powerful two-fisted punch delivered to a butt or butts. See *atomic power punch*.

Double-handed cheek-lock
Particularly brutal and effective butt-wrestling hold.

Ed Kelly
Pumpkin farmer who lives in *Marbleton.*

Eleanor Sterne
Ferocious *butt-fighter,* dedicated to destroying the *Great White Butt* after it killed her mother in a surprise attack on a family picnic when Eleanor was only four. Daughter of legendary *butt-hunter Silas Sterne.*

E-mission
Task or project undertaken by a *butt-fighter.* Not to be confused with "emission," which is something else entirely (see *fart*).

Ex-Mutant Barf Lord
Mutant Barf Lord that has been sucked into a *vacuum cleaner* and converted to a thin, watery puddle of blood and rotting flesh in the process.

False butt
Silicon-based imitation butt. May be *self-wiping.*

Fart
A small explosion between the legs. The exact size, duration, and intensity of the explosion, however, will vary depending on various factors including age, weight, and diet of the individual. Highly flammable. Avoid.

Fate
Another word for *accident.*

Final Conflict, The
The ultimate showdown between butts and humans in the battle for *world buttination.* See *Buttageddon.*

Flicker, The
Legendary *butt-fighter* highly skilled in the art of towel-to-butt combat. Member of the world's first butt-fighting team, *Mabel's Angels.*

Forker, The
Legendary *butt-fighter* highly skilled in the art of fork-to-butt combat. Member of the world's first butt-fighting team, *Mabel's Angels.*

Future present
The present moment that you will experience in a future moment. See *past future present, past present, present, present present.*

Giant arseteroid
Super-big *arseteroid* thought responsible for ending the reign of the *Great White Buttosaurs* sixty-five million years ago.

Giant brown blob
Gigantic, brown, and bloblike. Avoid.

Giant-brown-blobbification
To be completely engulfed by a *giant brown blob.* To be avoided at all costs. See *Blob-boy.*

Giant mutant blowfly
Adult form of *giant mutant maggot*. Avoid.

Giant mutant maggot
Larval form of *giant mutant blowfly*. Avoid.

Giant mutant zombie blowfly
Adult form of *giant mutant zombie maggot.* Virtually inde-structible. Avoid.

Giant mutant zombie maggot
Zombie-buttified giant mutant maggot. Avoid.

Great Unwiped Butt, The
See *Stenchgantor*.

Great White Butt, The
A rogue butt regarded by many as the most evil butt in the *univarse*. There are many theories about its origins. Some believe it to be a mutant butt created as a side effect of nuclear testing in the Pacific. Eric Von Dunnycan, in his book *Chariots of the Butts*, claimed that the Great White Butt was a space traveler who arrived on Earth thousands of years ago. Others believe the Great White Butt has been around for even longer and that it dates back one hundred fifty million years to the Jurassic period. Avoid.

Great White Buttosaur
The largest and most obnoxious of all the Buttosaurs. Probably the first land-dwelling butts to emerge from the *Sea of Butts*. Avoid.

Great Windy Desert, The
A blistering hot, terrifying wilderness devoid of all life except for *needleweeds, stinkants,* and *Ned Smelly.*

Henry
Zack Freeman's middle name.

Hokey Pokey
A really stupid dance, but quite good for amusing small children. Also good for sending *zombie butts* into a mysterious trance that enables you to pretty much lead them anywhere. Avoid unless you are a small child — or a parent desperately trying to amuse a small child — or your town is about to be overrun by zombie butts.

Holy buttrimony
A state of wedded bliss between two butts.

James and Judi Freeman
Zack Freeman's parents. Top-secret interplanetary *butt-fighters* who work undercover as musicians in the wind section of an orchestra.

Junior Butt-fighters' League
An organization dedicated to the early identification of young people with butt-fighting potential. Offers butt-fighting clinics, training camps, a national butt-fighting competition, and guest speakers. Contact the organization in your nearest capital city.

Kicker, The
Legendary *butt-fighter* highly skilled in the art of foot-to-butt combat. Member of the famous *B-team*.

Kisser, The
Exceptionally charming *butt-fighter* highly skilled in the art of lip-to-butt combat. Less inclined to physical violence than the other members of the *B-team*, the Kisser was no less effective a butt-fighter, however, thanks to his formidable charm and lethal "kiss of death." Buttnapped and brainwashed by butts, he became a secret butt sympathizer and not only sabotaged the B-team's butt-fighting *E-missions*, but ultimately attempted to kill its members. See *Mutant Maggot Lord, The*.

Mabel Freeman
Zack Freeman's grandmother, aka *the Pincher*.

Mabel's Angels
The world's first butt-fighting team, consisting of *the Flicker, the Forker,* and founding member *Mabel Freeman, the Pincher*.

Mabeltown
Large country town named in honor of *Mabel Freeman* in recognition of her efforts as the founding member of *Mabel's Angels*, credited with inventing modern butt-fighting.

Maggotorium
Enormous underground chamber. The cold, dark, and

moist environment provides ideal conditions for maggots, Maggot Lords, *giant mutant maggots, Mutant Maggot Lords,* and a range of other low-down scum-sucking parasites. Avoid.

Marbleton
Large country town named in honor of its annual marble-playing festival. The town is credited with the invention of modern marble-playing.

Maurice
Toadying servant of *the Prince*.

Methane madness
Delirium caused by exposure to high levels of methane. May cause hallucinations, visions, aggression, sudden mood swings, headaches, and vomiting. Can be relieved with pure oxygen.

Mittens
Mabel Freeman's cat.

Moby Dick
Fictional Great White Whale from the famous nineteenth-century novel of the same name by Herman Melville. See *Great White Butt, The*.

Mutant Maggot Lord, The
An exceptionally charming ex-human being (aka *the Kisser)* who, despite having his physical form, mutated beyond recognition as a result of prolonged exposure to

the extreme toxicity of a *brown lake* inside a *buttcano*, and then being eaten by *giant mutant zombie maggots* and regurgitated by *giant mutant zombie blowflies* and piecing himself together again, retains his persuasive powers.

Mutant Mutant Zombie Blowfly Barf Lord, The
See *Mutant Maggot Lord, The.*

Mutant Barf Lord, The
See *Mutant Maggot Lord, The.*

Mutant Barf Lord puddle
Remains of the *Mutant Barf Lord* after escaping from the *vacuum cleaner*.

Nailgun Series 9000
A popular *butt-gun* that fires high-velocity nails at its target (usually a butt). The 9000 series was notable for the innovation of using rusty nails capable of delivering a shot of tetanus as well as intense pain.

Ned Smelly
Butt-fighter who lives in the *Great Windy Desert*. Instrumental in helping to derail the *Great White Butt*'s plan to gas the world by means of a deadly *buttcano*. Brilliant inventor of *Robobutt.*

Needleweeds
Weeds that look and feel like a cluster of sewing needles. The only plant tough enough to grow in the *Great Windy*

Desert. May be eaten, but can cause excessive body odor.

Nuclear wart-head
Rough lump with explosive power.

Origins of the Univarse, The
Controversial bestseller by *Sir Roger Francis Rectum* in which he sets forth his theory of *buttolution*.

Party pooper
1) Somebody who spoils the fun. 2) Popular party game for butts.

Past future present
A present moment that you experienced in the future but which is now in your past (Note: This is an extremely complex concept to get your head around and, to be honest, not really worth the trouble unless you're planning to do a lot of time travel in the near future. Or the near past. Or the distant future. Or the distant past, as the case may be.) See *future present, past present, present, present present.*

Past present
A present moment that you experienced in the past. See *future present, past present, present, present present.*

Perambulic merimbulator
The most important and complex component of a time machine, although it can be made from a tin can and an

old mattress spring if you are a brilliant inventor like *Ned Smelly*.

Percy Freeman
Zack Freeman's grandfather. Legendary *butt-fighter*, highly skilled in the art of toilet-paper-to-butt combat (aka *the Wiper*). Co-founder, along with *Mabel Freeman*, of modern butt-fighting. Unfortunately wiped out by *Stenchgantor, the Great Unwiped Butt*.

Pincher, The
Legendary *butt-fighter* highly skilled in the art of forefinger-and-thumb-to-butt combat. Founding member of the world's first butt-fighting team, *Mabel's Angels*.

Poopasaur
Big, lumbering, and deadly. Lives in marshes and primeval *cocobutt-tree* forests. Avoid.

Poopigator
Just like an alligator, except browner. And smellier. Avoid.

Prehistoric stinkant nest
Where *prehistoric stinkants* live. A typical colony can consist of up to 200,000 prehistoric stinkants and can have anywhere between 10,000 and 20,000 food and egg chambers. Avoid. See *stinkants*.

Prehistoric stinkants
Just like regular *stinkants* except much, much bigger. Avoid. See *prehistoric stinkant nest*.

Present
The present moment in which no past moments or future moments exist. See *future present, past future present, past present, present present.*

Present present
The present moment you are presently experiencing in the present moment. See *future present, past future present, past present, present.*

Prince, The
A butt with a very high opinion of itself. Toadying servant of the *Great White Butt.*

Robobutt
State-of-the-art robotic butt designed to look like a *Great White Butt.* Fully riveted reinforced steel cheeks. Turbo-assisted jet repulsion units. *Nuclear wart-head* equipped. Matter transport assisted entry and exit. Inside and outside voice options. Onboard tea- and coffee-making facilities. Also *self-wiping.* Invented by *Ned Smelly.*

Robospeak
To speak in a robotic manner.

Sea of Butts, The
A large inland sea teeming with aquatic butt-life. Many scientists believe that life on Earth originated in the Sea of Butts with single-cheek butt life forms.

Self-wiping
A highly desirable feature of both natural and artificial butts. See *false butt*.

Silas Sterne
Legendary *butt hunter* dedicated to hunting and killing the *Great White Butt*. Founder of *Silas Sterne's Butt-fighting Academy*.

Silas Sterne's Butt-fighting Academy
Founded by *Silas Sterne* in order to give rookie *butt-fighters* a solid grounding in the theory and practice of professional butt-fighting. It offers an initial three-month training course for a basic *butt-fighter's* certificate. Recruits can then go on to receive more advanced training and specialize in one or more particular butt-fighting techniques such as kicking, punching, and smacking.

Simulated butt-fighting
See *butt-fighting simulator*.

Sir Roger Francis Rectum
Author of *The Origins of the Univarse* — a controversial book in which Sir Roger set out his theory of *buttolution*. Also author of *What Buttosaur Is That?*

Smacker, The
Legendary *butt-fighter* highly skilled in the art of hand-to-butt combat. Member of the famous *B-team*.

S. McKerr's Bakery
Marbleton bakery run by S. McKerr. Famous for her ultra-big, ultra-soft buns.

Soap
A *butt-fighter's* best friend. (Note: The first rule of butt-fighting is to always wash your hands afterwards.)

Stenchgantor
Also known as the *Great Unwiped Butt,* it is the ugliest, dirtiest, wartiest, pimpliest, grossest, greasiest, hairiest, stinkiest butt in the entire world. Or, at least it was, until *Zack Freeman* outstenched it with a pair of very smelly socks. Avoid.

Stinkant juice
Thick greasy liquid obtained from *stinkants*. Used for a variety of purposes, most commonly as fuel for robotic butts and *butt-mobiles*. One of the most powerful fuel sources in the world. Highly sought after.

Stinkant-napped
To be kidnapped by *prehistoric stinkants*. Avoid.

Stinkants
Small red ants with a great big stink. The only creature tough enough to survive — and thrive — in the *Great Windy Desert*. Some varieties bite. May be eaten but can cause flatulence and serious body odor. See *prehistoric stinkant nest, prehistoric stinkants*.

Stinkbog
Area where a thick, sticky, stinky bog accumulates, trapping those animals, butts, and *butt-fighters* unlucky enough to fall into it and become preserved for future generations to laugh at. Avoid.

Stink Kong
Very large, very clumsy, very smelly, very stupid, very ugly *buttosaur*. Mortal enemy of the *Great White Butt*. Avoid.

Temporal navigator
Device used for navigating *butt-mobiles* through time.

Tricerabutt
Extraordinarily bad-tempered three-cheeked *buttosaur* with bony armor plating and a tusklike wart growing out of each cheek. Avoid.

Twin-tyrannosore-arse attack
Attack by two *tyrannosore-arses* working as a team. Avoid.

Tyrannosore-arse
Large, fierce, flesh-eating *buttosaur* notable for the extreme redness and soreness of its enormous cheeks. Avoid.

Univarse
Everything that you can possibly think of plus everything that you can't. There are many theories about how the univarse began, but the truth is that most of the theories are just that. Theories. All that can be said for certain is that in the beginning there was a butt.

Uranus
Planet 1.783 billion miles from the Sun. It has seventeen known moons and eleven rings. Uranus's surface is an ocean of liquid methane that gives the planet a beautiful blue color. (Note: Extreme caution must be taken with the pronunciation of this planet's name to avoid potential confusion and embarrassment.)

Vacuum cleaner
Electrical appliance that cleans surfaces by sucking dirt into a bag or plastic container. Also good for sucking up mutant puddles.

Wart-horns
Warts that have grown so big and hard that they've turned into tusks. Avoid. See *Tricerabutt*.

What Buttosaur Is That?
Respected fieldguide to identifying and classifying all forms of *buttosaurs*. Written, illustrated, and published by *Sir Roger Francis Rectum*.

Wiper, The
See *Percy Freeman*.

World buttination
Total domination of the world by butts.

Zack Freeman
A twelve-year-old boy who lived a perfectly ordinary life

until two months after his twelfth birthday, when his butt ran away. To his utter surprise he discovered that he was an extraordinarily talented *butt-fighter*. He immediately put this talent to good use by saving the world from total *butt-bliteration*. Twice. You can read all about his heroic deeds in *The Day My Butt Went Psycho!* and *Zombie Butts from Uranus!* His grandmother, *Mabel Freeman,* was the inventor of modern butt-fighting. His parents, *James and Judi Freeman*, were secret butt-fighting agents. And *Zack Freeman's butt* was the next best thing to a lethal weapon. Together Zack and his butt formed a crack butt-fighting team, and with the help of *Eleanor Sterne*, a fierce butt-fighter in her own right, they were practically unbeatable.

Zack Freeman's butt

Bad, disobedient, argumentative, opinionated, cheeky, brave, resourceful, smart, cowardly, sensitive, kind, mean, romantic, stupid, and very, very smelly.

Zack Freeman's parents

See *James and Judi Freeman.*

Zombie butt

A butt that is neither dead nor fully alive. Zombie butts feel no pain, have no thoughts or feelings, and possess incredible powers of regeneration, which make them almost impossible to destroy. Driven to zombie-buttify potential victims, their only known weaknesses are extreme heat and a fondness for the *hokey pokey*. Avoid.

Zombie-buttification

Parasitic attachment of a *zombie butt* to a victim's real (or artificial) butt. Turns the victim into an eating machine that exists for the sole purpose of making the zombie butt bigger and fatter than it already is. When the host is exhausted, the zombie butt will simply abandon him or her and move on in search of a new victim.

Zombie-buttified

See *zombie-buttification*.

Zombie-buttvasion

Invasion of a place — or entire planet — by *zombie butts*.

About the Author

Andy Griffiths is the best-selling author of the JUST series — *Just Joking!*, *Just Annoying!*, *Just Stupid!*, *Just Wacky!*, and *Just Disgusting!* — as well as the two previous novels in the butt trilogy, *The Day My Butt Went Psycho!* and *Zombie Butts from Uranus!* Andy lives in Melbourne, Australia with his wife and two daughters. He recently gained his basic butt-fighter's certificate from Silas Sterne's Butt-fighting Academy and hopes to become a professional butt hunter when he grows up.

FOR MORE NOSTRIL-BURNIN' FUN, JUST GET YOUR BUTT TO

WWW.SCHOLASTIC.COM/ANDYGRIFFITHS

- HOP TO SAFETY AND VICTORY IN THE ONE-AND-ONLY
ANDY GRIFFITHS GAME

- DISCOVER ANDY'S FAVORITE THINGS (LIKE FINDING **DIRTY TOOTHBRUSHES** AND ADOPTING THEM)

- READ **LAUGH-OUT-LOUD** EXCERPTS FROM SOME OF ANDY'S FUNNIEST BOOKS!